THE MYSTERY OF THE OBDURATE OUTCAST

THE THREE INVESTIGATORS

IN

THE MYSTERY OF THE OBDURATE OUTCAST

BY

ELIZABETH ARTHUR
& STEVEN BAUER

BASED ON CHARACTERS
CREATED BY ROBERT ARTHUR

Hollow Tree Press 2026

A HOLLOW TREE PRESS BOOK

Copyright © 2025
Elizabeth Arthur and Steven Bauer
Hollow Tree Press LLC

Jacket Concept Elizabeth Arthur
Jacket Design and Cover Art
© 2025 Hollow Tree Press LLC
Cover Art Pashur House

"The Three Investigators" ® & "???" ®
By Permission of Elizabeth Arthur

Published in the United States of America
All Rights Reserved

ISBN PB:978-1-965321-42-3
ISBN HC: 978-1-965321-43-0
ISBN EB: 978-1-965321-44-7

CONTENTS

1

A Present From The Past

Jupiter Jones yawned, rolled over, and peeked at his watch. He stared in disbelief. It was eight-fifteen already? How had that happened? It seemed he'd just gone to sleep a minute ago instead of − what? − ten hours? He sat up, rubbed his eyes, and put his bare feet flat on his bedroom floor. Although he still had plenty of time before he was due to meet his friends Bob Andrews, Pete Crenshaw, and Mallory MacLeod at their new Three Investigators Headquarters around the corner in the Salvage Yard, he did need to get going now.

For weeks he'd been sleeping longer than he'd expected to. Aunt Mathilda said it was normal − growing boys needed their rest. But he hadn't taken her word for it. He'd done his research, and she was right; it was scientific fact. Between the ages of fourteen and sixteen you needed to sleep more, eat more, and make sure your pants were long enough. He wondered how tall he was going to get.

Maybe taller than Uncle Titus, who was close to six feet. How tall had Jupiter's father been? Jupiter didn't know. His mother and father had died when he was still an infant, and since Jupiter's father Claudius had been much younger than his half-brother Titus, if Jupiter were to come right out and ask his uncle how tall his father had been, Uncle Titus might not even know.

His uncle had very few photographs of Jupiter's father, and in all of them, his father was sitting in a chair or posing on one knee or driving a car; there was no way to gauge how tall he'd been. He'd died at the age of just 27. Jupiter was still not yet 16, but even so, he felt he was starting to look like the person he would grow up to be — a very different person from the one who had once played a character named Baby Fatso on television. He wished someone could tell him whether he looked like his father, or sounded like him, or acted like him, or resembled him in some other way. It would give him a connection to his father he'd never had.

In the bathroom, he brushed his teeth and washed his face. Then, back in his bedroom, he put on a pair of khaki pants and a long-sleeved button-down shirt. As always, he made his bed, with crisp hospital corners. It was a satisfying task, leaving his bedroom tidy.

He stretched and went to the window, which looked down on Red Gate Rover and the back of the Salvage Yard fence. The brightly-colored mural painted on it seemed a little faded in the early morning light. Undoubtedly his aunt and uncle were already at work. They were usually up, as his aunt said, with the birds.

As he stared down at the Salvage Yard, he wondered if Mallory was already sorting and categorizing, taking pictures and writing copy about the items Uncle Titus had bought. She'd said she wanted to get some hours of work in today before a new case presented itself.

What would that be? he wondered. He thought about how the first two cases of the summer had involved his friends' families. Bob's father had gotten caught up in the first one, while Pete's mother had started the second one off, and while he was thrilled that The Three Investigators had managed to help Pete's aunt and uncle, both cases had left him feeling a little bit more of an orphan than usual.

He knew, of course, that this was silly. He was very lucky to have his Uncle Titus and his Aunt Mathilda, as well as the bits of his extended family he'd discovered two summers ago up in Jackson – his second cousins Harper and Luke, his great aunt and her son. But the fact was that Bob was very close to his father. Aside from the two of them being very good friends, Malcolm Andrews was a mentor and role model for Bob, and although they looked somewhat different, they had a huge amount in common.

As for Pete, although he looked a lot like his father Martín, and they were both athletic and physical, he actually had a lot more in common with his mother Valeria. They were both intuitive and emotional and led with their hearts. Pete was very close to his mother.

It wasn't that Jupiter didn't love his aunt and uncle; he loved them a lot and appreciated them for what they'd accomplished, and for the way they'd let him grow up to be who he was. When he was younger, it hadn't bothered him at all that they were so different from him, but it bothered him a little now.

No, that wasn't quite right. It didn't bother him that they were different. What bothered him was that he didn't have someone in his life he got along with the way Bob got along with his father and Pete with his mother. His great-aunt Dora's son John Pelletier was a

blood relation, if distant, but as a time management consultant, his interests were very different from Jupiter's — and besides, he lived almost six hours away.

Yes, he thought. John Pelletier's interests were very different from his. So were Aunt Mathilda's and Uncle Titus's. Aunt Mathilda seemed mainly interested in managing her rambunctious and overly-enthusiastic husband, and Uncle Titus was interested in his never-ending treasure hunt as he searched for salvage, always intent on the next great find.

If someone who didn't know him were to ask Jupiter what his interests were, exactly, what would he say? How would he describe them? He paused and pinched his bottom lip, staring out at the interplay of sun and shadow in the yard, the way it shifted as the breeze blew through. It made him think about how so much of life was complicated, illusory, difficult to pin down. If someone asked him, Jupiter thought he'd say that his interest lay in getting down to bedrock, in uncovering truth.

Yes, he thought, "uncovering" was the right word. "Discovering" would be entirely wrong. After all, as he'd come to understand, truth was truth. It couldn't be discovered — only revealed or understood. Well, maybe that would be going too far, actually. Sometimes truth had to be revised, as previously unknown information became available.

Still, what he would want to explain, if anyone were to ask him, was that truth was very stubborn. It didn't shift or change to fit the current fancy. It couldn't be tailored to support a particular ideology. It was intractable, unalienable, fixed.

Jupiter admired the ability Bob shared with his father to use language and to tell stories in order to convey complex ideas, and he also appreciated the way that Pete and his mother intuitively understood and responded to other people. But if he could have chosen a parent to be part of his life as he grew from childhood to adulthood, it would have been someone who shared with him a dedication to uncovering the truth.

Someone who shared his desire to get to the bottom of small questions like the ones The Three Investigators always tackled in their mysteries, but also someone who wanted to ask big questions, like what the nature of the world was – and, just as important, what was the best way for people to live in it.

Those were two very different questions, Jupiter reflected. The question about the nature of the world was best answered by scientists, but the question about how best to live in it was the province of philosophers and theologians. And while Jupiter hoped that by the time he applied to college he'd have figured out which of the two questions interested him the most, as he headed downstairs, he thought that now was not the best time to decide. Besides, he was hungry. As it turned out, growing boys not only needed sleep but food as well.

The kitchen was empty, as he had expected. The coffee maker had been turned off, with a small amount of coffee still in the carafe. His aunt had left Jupiter a note wishing him a good morning and a plate of pancakes for him to heat up in the microwave. He felt a rush of warmth. He felt very grateful to her for both the note and the plate, and he thought how lucky he was, really. His aunt and uncle might have different interests from his, but they had always made him feel safe and well loved.

As the pancakes heated up, Jupiter got himself a glass of milk and turned on the small television his uncle had recently moved to the kitchen. Uncle Titus liked to watch the 6 o'clock local news while they ate dinner, followed by the national news at 6:30. At first Jupiter had thought that dinnertime was better spent talking, but with his uncle's coaxing he'd gotten interested.

Now, he settled down at the table with his pancakes and stared at the screen.

"It's a beautiful day in southern California! Welcome to KRBT's Morning Report. I'm John Welkhorn, joined as always by Erika Kaison."

Jupiter thought the term "meat puppet" was distasteful, but he understood why people used it. John Welkhorn was not a reporter; he was a telegenic, deep-voiced, well-coiffed forty-year-old with a face so untroubled Jupiter was sure the man had never had a thought in his life. His torso, clad in a starched white shirt, a red tie, and a blue sports jacket, jutted above a brown formica desk. He had a bunch of papers before him, which Jupiter always found amusing, since all he was doing was reading from a teleprompter.

John Welkhorn's co-anchor was an African-American woman with wavy shoulder-length hair and pearl earrings, wearing a sleek red dress. She took off her tortoise-shell glasses and leaned forward earnestly. Jupiter thought she looked slightly alarmed.

"Californians woke up to a startling political development," she said. "Senator Jack

Hayden is dead at 79. Senator Hayden, who hailed from Santa Monica, succumbed to a heart attack last evening. He has represented California in the United States Senate for the last twenty-four years, and he was up for re-election in November. John?"

"Thank you, Erika," John Welkhorn said, self-importantly. "Senator Hayden's sudden and unexpected demise has thrown the Senate race, now less than four months away, into chaos. For more, let's turn to María Flores in Santa Monica."

María Flores was a reporter Jupiter had begun to notice. She seemed more serious than many of her peers and her on-air commentary tended to be focused and articulate. This morning she looked a bit flustered. She held her microphone close to her mouth and spoke into it urgently.

"Thank you, John," she said. "The shock waves are just beginning to reach California's political establishment. Senator Hayden had his detractors, but he was a familiar and well-loved figure to many. At 79, he was determined to seek another six-year term, though many of his critics had decreed that it was time for him to step down. Although his doctors repeatedly claimed that he was healthy and up to the task, there were persistent rumors that he had begun to slip a little cognitively."

Jupiter hadn't been paying much attention to the senatorial race, but he'd noticed several hyperkinetic commercials put out by Hayden's campaign – Hayden playing with his two Golden Retrievers, hiking up Mount Tamalpais, kicking a soccer ball around with his grandchildren. They'd used inspiring patriotic music and otherworldly lighting to cast Hayden as an indispensable elder statesman while conveying the message that the senator was in excellent physical condition.

He didn't seem like the sort of man who would suffer a sudden heart attack, Jupiter thought. But then again "underlying conditions" were not always evident, and if the senator had had any, his campaign was not about to advertise them.

"But his re-election campaign was in full swing," Flores continued. "He was up in the polls and had accumulated a huge war chest, much of it raised through small donations from ordinary Californians. This is, of course, a terrible shock to his family, and our hearts go out to them. Back to you, John."

On the Morning Report, Welkhorn had turned to Erika Kaison and was gazing at her

raptly. She was talking about the rumors of Hayden's faltering mental capacity.

"The senator's death comes at a time when he had been less and less in public view," she said. "After a well-publicized run of gaffes − including a recent occasion when he couldn't seem to recall the name of his fellow senator from California − Senator Hayden had gone missing, sending aides and stand-ins to a number of scheduled public appearances and even turning most of his fundraisers into virtual events, held over Zoom."

"I expect all that chatter will die down now that the man is dead," Welkhorn intoned somberly. "Attention will turn, as it should, to the question of who will now be the second senator representing Californians in the Capitol. With just four months until Election Day, will Governor Albright appoint a replacement or let the seat sit vacant?"

"Top party officials will certainly press Albright to appoint someone," Kaison said.

"Would that replacement be the party's candidate in the general election in the fall?" Welkhorn asked. "Or might someone other than the replacement run for a new term? This is a breaking story, and we will have to wait for developments, Erika." He looked directly at the camera and said, "Stay tuned."

Erika Kaison gave him a look that indicated she knew he was an idiot.

Jupiter picked up the remote and turned off the news. His scalp prickled — the odd sensation he often got when things were not as they appeared to be. While Jupiter was intrigued by the news of Hayden's sudden death, he was not really surprised.

About a week ago, he and his aunt and uncle had seen, on the 6 o'clock local news, a report that Hayden had been taken to Oceanview Hospital in Santa Monica with a broken foot.

He had supposedly suffered this injury after tripping and falling while throwing a ball for his dogs, and Jupiter, Aunt Mathilda, and Uncle Titus had seen news footage of Hayden walking out of the hospital, waving to the cameras, and wearing a large black boot — a walking cast that rose above his ankle. The reporter had told her listeners that, according to medical reports, Hayden had a hairline fracture of the metatarsals and would be wearing the cast for four to six weeks. It would take that long for the bones to heal, especially for a 79-year-old.

Jupiter had thought little of this at the

time and felt nothing except a vague sort of sympathy for anyone who would have to lug around something as big and uncomfortable-looking as that walking cast. So he had been startled when, three days later, he and his aunt and uncle had seen some more coverage of Senator Hayden.

This time he was on his way to attend one of his very rare in-person fundraisers, and as he approached the limousine that would transport him, he smiled widely and waved to reporters, and Jupiter saw that Hayden was no longer burdened by the walking cast. He was wearing a pair of very normal, if highly polished, shoes, and he seemed to be walking just fine.

This, Jupiter had thought, was both strange and suspicious. It was as though the supposed injury had never happened. As Jupiter immediately pointed out to his aunt and uncle, if Hayden seemed to have recovered almost overnight from a hairline fracture of the metatarsals, then he had never truly injured his foot in the first place. So why had he gone to the hospital?

Jupiter had pointed out to his aunt and uncle that in all probability Hayden had gone for a reason that had nothing to do with his foot, but given the public scrutiny that attended political figures' medical conditions, Hayden's handlers had cooked up a cover story so that no one would be worried that there was something more serious wrong with the senator.

Uncle Titus had teased him, saying he didn't need to be an investigator every minute of his life, but Jupiter was now sure he'd been right – Senator Hayden had almost certainly been treated for something more serious than some broken bones in the foot. Otherwise it would be an amazing coincidence that he had actually died seven days later. What had he and his handlers wanted to keep secret?

Jupiter put his dishes in the dishwasher and headed for HQ2. It had been Mallory's idea to call their new Headquarters HQ2, and their old Headquarters HQ1, but they all liked the names a lot. As Jupiter let himself through the gate and began walking across the Salvage Yard, he saw Leif and Magnus Haldorrson, the business's resident carpenters, emerge from their workshop and wave at him.

"Jupiter!" Leif called. "We need to talk to you."

This was a surprise. Usually Leif and Magnus were busy all day with the various projects and commissions they got from Aunt

Mathilda and Salvage Yard customers, and sometimes Jupiter didn't see them from one day to the next.

Both were tall, white-blond, and wiry. They could hardly look more like brothers, Jupiter thought, but their dispositions could not be more different. Leif was optimistic, cheerful, full of energy, and able to see the good in almost anything, while Magnus was like Pooh's friend Eeyore, generally gloomy and expecting the rain clouds to cover the sun. Jupiter was always glad to see the brothers, who he'd gotten quite fond of.

"We just got a call from our father," Magnus said. "He asked us to see if you, Pete, Bob, and Mallory could come to our house in Palisade Point soon."

It was an even bigger surprise that Dr. Haldorrson, a well-regarded orthopedic surgeon, wanted to consult with The Three Investigators.

"You mean this morning?" Jupiter said. "I'll have to ask the others, but I think it's possible." He had met Dr. Haldorrson several times but didn't know him well. "What's the problem?"

"Father wants you to conduct an investigation into one of his patients. Someone famous."

Magnus nodded gloomily. "Famous people can be very dangerous," he said. "And this might involve a malpractice suit."

"Oh, nonsense!" Leif said, punching his brother on the arm.

"Did your father say anything else?" Jupiter asked.

"No," Magnus said, "and that's what worries me. I'll drive the four of you over to the house if your aunt says I can go."

"I'm sure she will," Jupiter said. "Remind me. Where does your father work?"

"He has a practice in Santa Monica," Leif said, "and he's based at Oceanview Hospital."

"Oceanview Hospital?" Jupiter said, surprised. Wouldn't it be odd if Dr. Haldorrson had something to tell The Three Investigators that involved the death of Senator Hayden? Or if he had some information about the supposed broken bones in the senator's foot? It did seem like quite a coincidence.

"I'm meeting everyone soon," Jupiter said, "and I'll let you know if we can all make it."

"Good," Magnus said. "I'll ask your aunt if I can drive you."

"Thanks, Jupiter," Leif said as he and his brother headed back to their workshop and Jupiter continued on toward HQ2. What could the mystery be that Dr. Haldorrson wanted to tell them about? he wondered. He'd almost gotten through the outdoor workshop to the side door leading to the new Headquarters when Mallory burst out of the shed where she'd been working. So she'd made it in early, Jupiter thought. She'd been working while he'd been sleeping late. She looked excited.

"Jupiter!" she called. "I've been watching for you."

She came running up to him, carrying under her arm what looked like some sort of metal headpiece. It was dark and tarnished and a bit rusted. More than excited, she seemed filled with joy at what she was about to tell him. Her face was radiant; her red hair seemed to glow in the morning light. She almost stumbled over herself trying to get the words out.

"There's so much junk in the shed I'm working in," she said, "but you just will *not* believe what I found!"

Jupiter knew that Mallory was fond of armor, and very knowledgeable about it, as well as about ancient weaponry. In fact, the very first time Pete and Bob had met her, it was because his uncle had put an imitation suit of armor outside the Salvage Yard gate as an eye-catcher and Mallory, who'd been riding her bike past it, had stopped to stare at it in dismay.

"A helmet of some kind?" he asked.

"Oh, much, much better than that," Mallory said. She pulled a stained white envelope out of the helmet and thrust the envelope toward him. "It's a letter from your father!"

"My father?" Jupiter said, astonished. He stared down at the envelope she had handed him, stunned. Just this morning he'd been wondering how tall his father was. Now this! The envelope had the name *Septimus Halfpenny* written on it, but no address or stamp. It had never been mailed.

"Septimus Halfpenny," Jupiter said thoughtfully.

"At first I wasn't even sure it was a name. It's certainly unusual enough," said Mallory.

"Septimus from the Latin," Jupiter said, "meaning 'seventh.' I've read that when families were much larger, it was the name often given to the seventh son. I imagine the surname pegs him as having British ancestry. What does the letter say?" Jupiter asked.

"Well, it seems that Septimus Halfpenny was a special friend of your father's, and your father was sending him a birthday present," Mallory said. "From what I can gather, the letter was written when you were a baby and living with your parents in Toronto."

"How did it get *here*?" Jupiter asked.

"I don't know," Mallory said. "But maybe it came with all your parents' stuff after the car accident. Your uncle was the next of kin. I think the letter and helmet must have never been sent because your father died before he could mail them. Look at the helmet!"

She handed it to him.

"It's an authentic Spanish morrión," Mallory said. "I'm almost positive. A conquistador's helmet from the 16th or 17th century."

Jupiter was dumbfounded. "He was sending this to his friend as a birthday present?" he asked.

Mallory nodded. She was smiling so widely – so happy to have brought him something from his father – that he thought her face must hurt. He looked down at the morrión and turned it over in his hands. It was hard to believe that over five hundred years ago a Spanish soldier who had come to the Americas in search of gold and treasure had worn this on his head. It was heavy, made of iron, Jupiter supposed, and quite thick, with a round dome, a wide curved brim, and a crest, like a rooster's comb, from front to back.

The exterior had a dark mottled patina, slightly dented here and there, and engraved with an arabesque design of intertwining flowering vines. The crest was three inches tall.

"There would have been plumes as well," Mallory said. "But that's not really the point. The point is that your father sounds – well, he sounds great. Go ahead, read the letter. Read it aloud, if you want."

Jupiter carefully took the letter out of the envelope. The handwriting was spiky and interesting, very forceful and direct, no curlicues or loops or decorations. He began reading.

"'My dear Septimus,'" he said. "'Happy birthday, old chap. Now that you are as old and wise as I am – ha! – we can perhaps together start to unravel some of the secrets of this life on which we are jointly embarked. It is, as you know, a quest that began with the most ancient civilizations, among them your beloved Maya, whose mathematicians and astronomers solved so many mysteries here in the Americas at the time the Romans were thriving in Europe. If only their codices had survived!'"

"I wonder what codices are," Jupiter said.

"I looked it up this morning," said Mallory, "after I found the letter. The Maya wrote down their discoveries in hieroglyphics, in folding books, on paper made from tree bark. They were supposedly savages because they weren't Christians, so this priest named Diego de Landa, the so-called Bishop of the Yucatán, ordered the codices to be burned in 1562. He said they were the work of the devil."

"All of them?" Jupiter asked, aghast.

Mallory nodded. "It seems most soldiers followed de Landa's orders. Though one soldier tried to save as many as he could. Your father mentions him."

Jupiter turned back to the letter.

"'The Spaniards and the Catholic Church have much to answer for,'" he went on. "'In fact, the enclosed may well have been worn by one of those book-burning barbarians, but I harbor a small hope that it belonged to your hero, Juan de Pistrano. After all, it was your interest in him that spurred your collection of relics from the conquest.

"'The enclosed morrión is, I think, authentic. I am not entirely sure, but it has the right feel. I found it at a flea market here in

Toronto for the unbeatable price of $25, and I thought you might want it to add to your collection. I wish it could be a lost codex, but I have not seen one in all of Toronto!

"'The helmet is my birthday gift to you, and I request only that when I next come back to California in a few months that you put it on your high-browed head and model it for me.

"'Until then, I remain your most faithful friend, Claudius.'"

Although Jupiter wasn't normally lost for words, as he folded the letter and tucked it carefully back into its envelope, he was literally speechless. He felt as if it was *his* birthday, suddenly – because although The Three Investigators had discovered a lot of lost or forgotten or hidden objects of value in the time since they'd set up their firm, they had never found one that meant so much to him personally.

And not just because there was something about the way the letter was written which reminded him of himself – at least as he might be twelve years in the future – but it could be seen as the first and most important clue in a sort of treasure hunt – the final prize of which would be finding this Septimus Halfpenny, and introducing himself as Claudius Jones's son!

An Eight-Sided House For The
Seventh Son

Ten minutes later, Mallory was sitting with Jupiter in The Three Investigators' outdoor workshop, explaining everything that had happened that morning that had led to the discovery of the letter and the Spanish morrión.

She'd gotten to the Salvage Yard at seven o'clock sharp, slipping through the wrought-iron gates and closing them behind her. She'd been spending so much time working as The Three Investigators' Special Consultant that she'd decided that starting early was the only way she could fit in the hours of work she'd promised Aunt Mathilda.

Aside from the sound of an occasional passing car or the plangent calls of a mourning dove, it had been quiet. She'd pushed her bike to the shed where she'd been sorting for the past few days.

It was the oldest and grungiest shed in the whole of the Salvage Yard, full of bits and pieces that Uncle Titus and Aunt Mathilda had stuffed there over the time they'd been in business. Though Mallory had been working for the Joneses for the past two years, she'd never been in it before.

In fact, when she went in, she'd suspected she was the first person to have set foot in it for quite a while. Mice had had a field day, chewing the corners of cardboard boxes, making nests of old fabric. Clouds of dust rose whenever she moved a box. She'd decided that this shed was where all the unfixable, unlikable, unusable, and unsaleable items that Titus Jones had gathered in his long career as a junk dealer had gone to die, and for a while she'd thought that the best way to proceed would be to park a large dumpster right next to the shed and then ask Leif and Magnus to pitch everything in it.

However, luckily, in the end she had steeled herself to take each item, one at a time, and consider it carefully, sorting and describing and cataloguing. About three-quarters of what she uncovered was worthless, put at one end of the shed to be thrown away. But she'd found some good stuff hidden among all the bad.

A number of old 45 rpm records that looked as though they'd never been played; a jacketless second impression of the first American edition of *The Hobbit*; a small marble bust of a woman with wide eyes and flowing hair.

Though she hadn't told Jupiter *this*, she had actually been oddly distracted – pitching and sorting with increasing impatience as she thought about her mother. When they'd first moved from Scotland to Rocky Beach after the death of Mallory's father, Mallory had been pretty sure that, although her mother would be happy in her old hometown, she herself would be miserable. Ironically it hadn't turned out that way at all.

She'd ridden by the Salvage Yard the day that Uncle Titus had posed that ghastly fake suit of armor by the gates, and after she'd met the boys, everything had changed. Meanwhile, her mother had gotten more and more unhappy. Last year she'd dated some costume designer who Mallory thought was an idiot.

Thank God, the relationship had now ended – but Mallory was coming to understand that her mother wouldn't be truly happy until she got married again, and when, at breakfast that morning, her mother had told Mallory she was thinking of joining an online dating service, Mallory had been both revolted and understanding.

You'd think with forty million people in the state of California – and with twenty million of them men! – her mother might have been able to find someone to be happy with somewhere other than the Internet. But, of course, Mallory's father had been a tough act to follow.

In any case – as she *did* tell Jupiter! – she'd been absent-mindedly poking around in a cardboard box full of old newspapers when, quite unexpectedly, she'd found the Spanish morrión. A jolt had run through her. From the moment of discovery, she'd been on tenterhooks, waiting for Jupiter to appear. Now she was gratified beyond words by the way her lucky find had affected him.

"From the moment I took it out, I was sure it was the real thing," she said. "I looked up morrións online. It's worth about $3500, I think. That's not a fortune, but it's still a lot more than most of what I find every day. And it was also a lot more intriguing, with the envelope stuffed inside. All it had on it were the words 'Septimus Halfpenny.' The glue had dried up and the envelope flap was open, but I'm pretty sure I wouldn't even have opened it if it hadn't been for the words on the envelope."

Jupiter nodded gravely. "Perhaps we can track down this Septimus Halfpenny," he said.

"If so, I'd like to deliver his birthday present in person. It might be sixteen years late, but I think he'd still appreciate it."

Mallory wasn't sure, but she suspected that Jupiter harbored the idea that his father's friend might turn out to be someone he could have a relationship with – someone who might even become a sort of surrogate father. She hoped, for his sake, that turned out to be true, but she knew from bitter experience it didn't always work that way. The previous summer she and her mother had gone to visit a cousin of her father's in British Columbia, and she'd harbored similar fantasies. She'd liked the guy all right, but nothing had really come of it.

"Why don't we go into Headquarters," she said, "and I can look him up online?"

They entered HQ2 through the double doors that led from the outdoor workshop. Mallory was struck again, as she was every time she walked in, at how glorious the transformation of the old shed was. Above her the ceiling opened up to four long dormer windows in each of the building's sides and, at the very top, a cupola. The interior was spacious, light, and bright, and its four quadrants – informal and formal seating areas, office, and kitchen – gave them everything they could ever want. It was a workspace, a reception area for guests, and a clubhouse.

She and Jupiter had just settled down in their hang-out area when the front door opened and Pete and Bob burst in.

"Hey guys," Pete said. "Good morning!" Mallory was glad to see he was his usual ebullient self.

"Hey yourself," Mallory said. "Look what I found."

She held up the morrión and Pete stared at it in amazement.

"What *is* that?" he asked.

"It's a Spanish conquistador's helmet," Jupiter said. "Mallory thinks it's the real thing."

Pete picked it up and stared at it. He seemed to have a little trouble figuring out which was the front.

"Can I try it on?" he asked excitedly.

"Sure," Mallory said. "I don't think you can hurt it."

Pete lowered it over his head. It was big for him. The bowl was very deep and the rim came right to his eyebrows. He looked a little lost in it.

"This guy's head was huge!" Pete said. "How old is it?"

"About five hundred years," Mallory

said.

"Maybe it belonged to one of my ancestors!" Pete said.

"Your ancestors?" Mallory said.

"Sure," Pete said. "Mexicans have all sorts of mixed up blood lines – Indian and Spanish. And my mom's ancestors are Spanish. She thinks I'm the reincarnation of – "

"Yes," said Jupiter dryly. "One of the Boy Heroes of the Battle of Chapultepec. But look what else Mallory found. It's a letter from my father. He was going to send the helmet to a friend as a birthday present, but he died before he could." He handed the letter to Bob, who read it and handed it to Pete.

"Gee, Jupe," Bob said. "This is really amazing. And wonderful. And the letter's been in the Salvage Yard for all these years?"

"Yes," Jupiter said. "And if it hadn't been for Mallory, it might never have been found. It was in the shed with all the junk in it. The real junk, I mean. But Mallory knew the helmet must be authentic the minute she saw it. I'm always amazed at her ability to know what's real and what isn't, but never as much as now."

Mallory couldn't remember Jupiter ever saying anything about her in quite this way before – at least not in her presence – and she felt a rush of pleasure at the form his praise was taking. In fact, she felt that her finding the morrión and the letter would be something that tied her and Jupiter together forever. She hoped that if he were able to track down Septimus Halfpenny, he would prove as good a friend to Jupiter as he had to Jupiter's father.

Mallory pulled her laptop from her backpack and booted it up.

"There can't be all that many men named Septimus Halfpenny in the world," she explained when Pete looked at her inquiringly. "Why don't we use that people-finding search engine you can pay $5.00 to, to see if we can find an address or phone number?"

"Let's do it," said Jupiter, and Pete and Bob both nodded.

Mallory found the site, entered 'Septimus Halfpenny' in the search bar, and hit RETURN. Only two Septimus Halfpennys popped up, and since one was in his 80s and the other was in his 40s, there was no dispute about which of the two they should pay to find out more about. After Mallory used the firm's PayPal account, she got a bare-bones report.

This particular Septimus Halfpenny had a wife and a daughter who was now fifteen. He also had once had an address in Oxford, England and had recently lived in Palo Alto, California. There was no phone number or e-mail address, but there was a street address. He was now living — at least apparently — on the edge of Rocky Beach.

For a moment, Mallory could hardly speak, but at last she gathered herself together. "I've got his address, and although I doubt you'll believe this, he lives in Rocky Beach. We could get to his house on our bikes!" she said.

Pete almost shouted, "No way!" Bob laughed aloud with pleasure, and Jupiter looked stunned.

"He lives in Rocky Beach?" he sputtered.

"So far, it looks that way," Mallory said.

Going back to her usual search engine, Mallory typed the address she'd just found into the search bar. She was surprised once again — though this time, less so — when the first link she clicked on took her to a realtor's website. It appeared that the house Septimus Halfpenny was living in these days had been sold about nine months before, and the realtor had never taken the listing down. As Mallory stared at the exterior pictures, her eyes widened. She prided herself on her growing knowledge of architecture, but she'd never seen anything like the house she was currently staring at.

It had eight sides, rather than four, with a wide wooden porch that wrapped entirely around it and was supported by thin double Corinthian columns. Two sets of curving stairs swept up to the porch, which harbored a hothouse display of ferns and banana trees and lush exotic foliage that would have been the pride of any Victorian conservatory.

Above the porch roof was a second story with well-spaced windows looking out from each of the eight sides. Above was a third story whose walls were part of a splendid highly decorative curved dome, rising to a cupola, and above *that* a low parapet surrounded a tall ornamental spire. With the dome, and the slightly canted porch roof that surrounded the house like a wide fancy collar, the house looked like nothing so much as a human head.

"Look at his house!" she cried, holding the pictures up so that Jupiter, Pete, and Bob could see them. "It's like a head! Have you ever seen anything so fantastic?"

Fantastic was one word for it, Mallory thought, but it was also flamboyant, implausible, whimsical, and altogether unbelievable. And it had been built on a bluff overlooking the Pacific Ocean! She was finding it difficult to believe that someone actually lived in a house like this one, and her already deep curiosity about the man who presumably did was notched up considerably.

"Wow!" Pete said. "Is that a real house or just a drawing?"

"It's real enough," Mallory said. She did a few more quick searches.

"Septimus Halfpenny appears to be renting it from the man who bought it last year. A rich aristocrat who lives in England. Lord Blackwood."

"An eight-sided house for Septimus the seventh," Jupiter said. "Maybe he knows something we don't!"

"If you add seven and eight together," Pete said, "you get fifteen. And we're all fifteen."

"Soon to be sixteen," Jupiter said. Everyone laughed.

"It says here on the realtor's site that it's one of only two remaining Fowler's Octagons in southern California," Mallory said. "Boy, I'd like to get inside that house."

When she looked up Fowler's Octagons, Mallory learned that a man named Orson Squire Fowler − a phrenologist and amateur architect − had published a book called *The Oc-*

tagon House, a Home for All in 1848, setting off a nationwide craze. The eight-sided house, Fowler claimed, let in the most light and air and was therefore the healthiest design for a family home.

"What's a phrenologist?" Pete asked.

"Someone who studies the human head," Mallory said, "and thinks its bumps and shape can tell you about a person's mental traits."

"You mean, bumps on the head can *mean* things?" Pete asked. Self-consciously he was feeling his scalp.

"Only if you're a phrenologist," Mallory said.

"It's pseudoscience," Jupiter said. "Totally fake."

"But you can see why someone like Fowler would want to build a house that looks like a head," Mallory said.

Just then the four of them spotted Uncle Titus walking along the edge of the outdoor workshop and Jupiter dashed out to intercept him. Mallory and the others followed. When Jupiter's uncle saw them all rapidly approach, he laughed. "What's this? Time for another puzzle?"

"No," said Jupiter tersely. "This morn-

ing, Mallory found an authentic Spanish morrión in the junk shed, and there was a letter
tucked inside it. A letter from my father, written
not long before he died. He was living in Toronto at the time, and he had bought the
Spanish morrión for a friend of his named Septimus Halfpenny. Do you remember my father
ever talking about a friend with that name?"

"I certainly do!" exclaimed Uncle Titus.
"Who could ever forget a name like *that*! I remember Claudius telling me that his name was
one of the first things that brought your father
and his friend together. Not only were both of
their names out of the ordinary, but they were
both the names of Roman emperors! Just like
mine," Titus added, trying to look modest.

"That's very interesting," said Jupiter.
"But did you ever meet the man? Do you know
where he went to school, or where he lived?"

Though Mallory might have been imagining it, she thought she sensed that Jupiter was
actually a little exasperated. He'd been living
with his uncle since before he had learned to
speak, and yet, in the almost-fifteen years that
had passed since he'd been delivered into his
aunt and uncle's arms, Uncle Titus had never
once thought to mention that one of his father's closest friends had been a man named

Septimus Halfpenny.

Uncle Titus shook his head. "After you came to live with us, we invited him to visit and see you, but he was just about to leave the States to teach at the university in Oxford, England. So it never happened. As far as I know he's still in England."

"He isn't," said Jupiter. "At least we don't think so. And since the man we've tracked down *did* live in Oxford once, I'm pretty sure he's my father's old friend. He also used to live in Palo Alto but it seems that for the last seven or eight months, he's actually lived in Rocky Beach. We didn't find a phone number or an e-mail, but we have his street address."

"In Rocky Beach?" exclaimed Uncle Titus incredulously. "Then why didn't he stop by and see us? Maybe it's because your aunt and I stopped sending him Christmas cards a long time ago now. We just thought that if he lived in England, there was very little chance we'd ever get to meet him. Well, now we will! If you don't have his e-mail address or phone number, why don't you write him a real old-fashioned letter, like the one your father wrote to him? If you put it in the mailbox on the corner in the next forty minutes, it should get to him today!"

"Really?" asked Pete.

"Well, hopefully," Uncle Titus said. "The postmistress recently told me that the new Rocky Beach system is almost guaranteed!"

"Let's go back into HQ2 then," said Jupiter. Once they were back inside, they all sat around the big table and Mallory opened her laptop again.

"Go ahead and dictate a letter to me," she said. "I'll use the firm's electronic letterhead. And I'll type as fast as I can."

"O.K.," Jupiter said. "Fix it if it needs fixing. And I'll keep it short."

He cleared his throat. "Dear Dr. Halfpenny," he began.

"My name is Jupiter Jones, and I am the son of your old friend Claudius Jones. My colleague Mallory MacLeod has just discovered a letter and birthday present my father was going to send to you fifteen years ago, right before he died, when I was still an infant. I've found your address online, and I'd very much like the opportunity to bring the letter and gift to you, and to meet you. Would that be possible?

"Alternately, if you liked, you could come to see me. Together with three of my friends, I run a small investigative firm in Rocky Beach.

The address and phone are above in the letterhead, and you could, of course, also send me an e-mail.

"I will very much look forward to hearing from you.

"Sincerely, Jupiter Jones."

He paused as Mallory finished furiously typing and looked from her to Pete to Bob. "How does that sound?" he asked.

"It's great, Jupe," Pete said. "Boy, is he going to be surprised!"

"I think it's just what the situation calls for," Mallory said. "Shall I read it aloud?" When Jupiter said yes, she did. She thought it was intriguing enough and short enough to make anyone interested. "Do you want to go ahead and send it?"

Jupiter bit his lip. She couldn't quite figure out what he was feeling other than nervousness at taking this step. For a moment, she thought he would second-guess himself and decide not to contact his father's old friend. But he nodded, and she printed out a copy of the letter while Jupiter took out an envelope, wrote the address on the front of it, and stamped it. Then the four of them ceremoniously walked out to the mailbox on the corner of the Salvage Yard's block so that Jupiter could deposit the letter in its maw.

It vanished with a clang like the clang of a Spanish morrión's visor, and Mallory hoped that when he got it, Septimus Halfpenny would write back soon. Even more, she hoped that he and Jupiter hit it off a lot better than *she* had hit it off with her father's cousin. Jupiter certainly deserved it.

Back in Headquarters – and just as Pete was launching into a discussion of what had just happened with Jupiter's uncle – Jupiter suddenly changed the subject completely.

"Let's sit down," he said. "I have something to tell you all."

Pete threw himself into a beanbag chair and Bob chose a butterfly chair. The four of them huddled close.

"Just before Mallory found me and showed me the helmet and the letter," Jupiter said, "I was talking to Leif and Magnus. Their father wants to consult with us on a case."

"Dr. Haldorrson wants to hire us?" Bob asked.

" 'Hire' may be too strong," Jupiter said. "Consult, I think. But by now, Magnus has presumably asked my aunt if he can drive the four of his to his house in Palisade Point to meet with his father. He wouldn't tell Leif and

Magnus what it was all about, except to say that it involved someone famous – a patient of his who might be bringing a malpractice suit.

"That's all I know so far," Jupiter said. "But since Senator Hayden, who died last night, was apparently a patient at Oceanview Hospital – where Dr. Haldorrson practices – I must say I wondered whether this might have something to do with that. Although Senator Hayden is certainly famous, I don't see how he could bring a malpractice suit after his own death! Though perhaps a family member could. And I do know that he was supposed to have broken the bones in his foot a little more than a week ago – when he was treated at Oceanview Hospital."

"Wow!" Pete said. "And Dr. Haldorrson is an orthopedic surgeon. So maybe this *is* that!"

"Maybe," said Jupiter. "But we won't know until we talk to him ourselves. I'll tell you one thing, though. Dr. Haldorrson must be feeling pretty desperate to want to consult with a bunch of teenage detectives. The times I've met him, he seemed much too straitlaced – and also too private – to want to share his troubles with young people like ourselves. So let's all be on our best behavior when we meet him."

Pete, Bob, and Mallory all nodded, and then Pete reached over to pick up the Spanish morrión and put it on his head again. It still looked too big for him — and always would! — and it made Mallory remember the picture of the Fowler's Octagon that looked so much like a human head. She was eager to meet the man who lived in it — if truth be told, a lot *more* eager to meet him than to drive to Palisade Point to see what was troubling Dr. Haldorrson.

Just then, however, Magnus appeared to ask if they were ready, and when Bob jumped to his feet rather eagerly, Mallory suddenly realized that *he*, at least, had a reason to look forward to the trip to Palisade Point — and her name was Freya!

Dr. Haldorrson Gives Them A Case

A little while later, on the way to the Haldorrson's house, Bob was sitting in the back seat of the Salvage Yard truck Magnus was driving, wedged between Pete and Jupiter. Why did he always wind up in the middle? Bob asked himself. In the Flex, it was sometimes uncomfortable, but the truck was worse. He shifted and stretched his back. His knees ached. He was just too agreeable, he thought, and he hated any kind of quarrel, even good-natured sparring with Pete and Jupe. He had to start being more assertive.

After all, that was what The Three Investigators were all about, wasn't it? They not only solved mysteries; they stood up against injustice. Not that sitting in the middle of the back seat was exactly unjust, but still − .

There were larger injustices in the world, Bob thought. His father had recently been attacked by an online mob, intent on getting him fired from his job for having written something quite true. In the end, they had failed to damage either his reputation or his livelihood, but other people weren't always so lucky.

Jupiter was staring out the window, deep in thought. Bob imagined he was thinking either about Septimus Halfpenny or the upcoming interview with Dr. Haldorrson. Knowing Jupe, it was probably the latter. However, Bob knew they'd soon be making a trip to that spectacular eight-sided house.

It was weird how their families had gotten mixed up with the first two cases of the summer. Now Jupiter's father's old friend had suddenly shown up on their doorstep. Not that visiting Septimus Halfpenny would turn into a case. But still, it was interesting the way their families had been proving more important than usual to their investigations this summer. And after all, Leif and Magnus were sort of like family, and their father *had* called them in on a case. Though all they knew about it so far was that it involved someone famous – and maybe a malpractice suit.

Bob thought about the last time they'd all gone to the Haldorrson's – when Leif had wanted to drop off a side table he'd repaired in the shop – and how great it had been to see Freya, their younger sister, who'd had a crush on Bob for almost two years now. He had to admit that, underneath all the other things he was thinking about, he was wondering whether he'd ever get up the courage to invite Freya to be his guest at the upcoming wedding of Charlotte Mitchell and Connor O'Malley in Ojai.

The wedding was just over a week away now, and if he was going to invite Freya, he'd better do it soon. Pete was taking Califia and he'd been quite energetic in trying to convince Bob to invite Freya. And given Pete's track record as a matchmaker – .

Bob reminded himself that he needed to be more assertive, that timidity never got anybody anywhere. But this unexpected trip to the Haldorrsons' was really putting the pressure on him. Should he ask her if he saw her? What would it mean if she said no? Or yes! But he thought that if he were going to do it, he'd never have a better chance than this afternoon – that is, if Freya were home.

Bob thought for a moment of trying to talk to Pete about this, but there was no way he could do that without Jupiter and Mallory overhearing. Or worse, Magnus. He decided to keep his thoughts to himself, especially since they were so close to Palisade Point by now.

As they pulled into the Haldorrsons' driveway and they all piled out, Bob saw that Freya was indeed home. She was out in the back of the house, watering the perennial border. In fact, she seemed to be watering the blue geraniums he'd given her two summers before on an impulse and that she'd planted in the garden. She hadn't heard the truck pull in.

"Hi, Freya!" Pete yelled. She turned abruptly, the spray from the watering wand creating a rainbow in the afternoon sunlight. She smiled and waved. Pete looked at Bob as if to say, *Go on*, and Bob walked over to where Freya was just turning off the water. The others followed him.

"Wow!" Bob said, looking at the geraniums. "They've really grown a lot!"

"They love it in our backyard," Freya said. "I've already divided them twice. You gave me one plant. Now there are six."

"I'm glad they're doing so well," Bob said. He wasn't much for signs and symbols, but the geraniums really were thriving.

"I'm glad you're all here," Freya said. "Father has been so worried the past few days, and he's never worried. He's usually so much like Leif, always in a good mood, always optimistic. But for a week or so he's been more like gloomy Magnus." She looked at her brother and smiled.

"Aha!" Magnus said. "He has at long

last seen the light. Or should I say the dark?"

"Come on," Freya said. "Let me take you inside."

Bob and the others followed her up the three stone steps to the front door. The house looked just as he remembered it, with its steeply pitched roof and its grayish-green siding and ornamental brown trim. Overhead, a small balcony off the front room on the second floor was lined with gaily painted flower boxes from which long trails of yellow-flowering vines hung.

The entrance hall opened to a living room on the left and a dining room on the right. Bob caught a glance of the painting on the dining room wall that they had come to see two summers ago – a painting of Freya's grandfather's friend Bjørn Kalberg. Both her grandfather and Kalberg had been members of the Norwegian Resistance during the Second World War, and in the portrait Kalberg was a falconer, a fierce falcon on his leather-gloved wrist. He remembered how helpful Freya had been, translating old letters from the Norwegian, in solving that case.

As Freya showed them into the living room, Dr. and Mrs. Haldorrson rose to their feet. They looked just as they had every other time Bob had met them – Dr. Haldorrson, handsome, wiry, and blond, like his sons, but with a trim reddish beard, Mrs. Haldorrson, apple-cheeked like her daughter, with a cheerful, open face.

"Welcome!" Dr. Haldorrson said. "Thank you for coming."

"It is very good of you," Mrs. Haldorrson said. "Can we get you something to drink?" Without waiting for an answer, she said, "Freya, there are sodas in the refrigerator."

Freya was soon back with cold drinks for everyone, just as they all had settled down and the small talk had ended.

As quiet settled over the room, Dr. Haldorrson cleared his throat. "I must start by saying that everything I tell you this afternoon is strictly confidential, and must be kept that way." He looked a little alarmed to be saying this, Bob thought, but Jupiter took it in stride.

"I can assure you," Jupiter said, "that all our clients can trust us to keep their information confidential. You can rely on it." He took out his wallet and gave one of The Three Investigators' business cards to Dr. Haldorrson. Pete sat forward expectantly. Bob knew from long experience that Pete considered the delivery of one of their cards a crucial step in every new case.

Dr. Haldorrson examined the card admiringly and then passed it to his wife, who looked at it and gave it to Freya.

"Oh!" Freya said. "Mallory, you're on the card now!"

At the end of the previous summer, Jupiter, Pete, and Bob had had new cards printed with Mallory's name at the bottom as Special Consultant.

"Yes," Mallory said, smiling faintly. "I'm official."

"Good for you," Mrs. Haldorrson said.

"All right, then," Dr. Haldorrson said. "I guess you all know that I'm an orthopedic surgeon specializing in hip replacements. Well, the problem I want to talk with you about started because a patient came to me asking me to replace both of his hips. The thing is, there's absolutely nothing wrong with either of them. They're perfectly healthy specimens, no wear and tear, no arthritis. But it seems he's part of a movement called transhumanism, and he wants to get new hips now in case his hips might give out at some point in the future."

"Wow!" Pete said. "That's very weird."

"It certainly is," said Dr. Haldorrson. "And because the patient is very well-known in

California − and very rich − he seems to think he can just get me to do something I have no intention of doing. I don't know if you've ever heard of the Orion Rigby estate? It's on the ocean in Santa Monica, and this man bought it lock, stock, and barrel."

Bob *had* heard of Orion Rigby. Probably everyone had, in southern California. He'd been an eccentric and extraordinarily wealthy industrialist who'd amassed a fortune in the second half of the 19th century, and in 1907 he'd built an estate called Europa. He'd imported several buildings that had originally been built in various countries overseas and then dismantled stone by stone and reconstructed in California.

Rigby had been not only vastly rich but extremely eccentric, since he'd bought the acreage on the sea outside Santa Monica in order to build an estate where he could pursue his interest in spiritualism. If Bob was remembering correctly, he'd believed that the dead were able to communicate with the living − usually through the intercession of an intermediary, a medium. In a psychic trance, the medium was able to receive and transmit messages to the living from − as they said − beyond the grave.

But Rigby had also been interested in table-tipping − wherein spirits moved furniture − and automatic writing, in which the medium would take dictation from the dead. In séances, the medium would ask the spirits questions and then would repeat the answers to a rapt audience.

Because of Rigby's interest in talking with the dead, the two buildings he'd imported from Europe had both been purported to be haunted.

"Your patient bought the Orion Rigby estate?" Jupiter asked curiously.

"Yes," said Dr. Haldorrson. "And he turned it into an organization called The Institute for Eternal Consciousness. Before he founded the institute, he was what they call an 'influencer' in the realms of wellness and mindfulness and self-care and self-empowerment − all those New Agey concepts. He gave TED talks and lectures about transhumanism, and how human beings are just around the corner from becoming half human and half machine − how any day now people will basically be able to build new bodies for themselves.

"He has literally millions of followers on social media platforms like Instagram and Facebook," Dr. Haldorrson went on. "He's like a cult leader with a huge dispersed cult. Still, needless to say, as a doctor, my first rule is to do no harm, and all surgery has risks. Why would I cut out his healthy hips and replace them with metal ones?"

Freya suddenly spoke up. "Father won't tell you this himself," she said. "But he's the best. People come to see him from all over. His surgeries take less time and his patients get better more quickly."

"Freya," Dr. Haldorrson said, raising his hand in protest.

She looked fiercely proud of her father and fierce in his defense. She really was great, Bob thought. And very pretty.

"No, it's true, Jens," Mrs. Haldorrson said. "If these young people are going to help you, they should know. Especially because this man demands that the surgery be done by you because he knows how splendid you are."

Dr. Haldorrson looked almost embarrassed by what a good surgeon he was. He spread his hands before him as if to say, *What can you do?*

"But it's not just his hips," he explained. "He told me he expects to get all his joints replaced, one by one, by other specialists, so that there's no wear and tear on his body as he gets older. At first I could hardly believe what he was telling me, but he went on to say he takes huge numbers of supplements and legally prescribed drugs, and eats a very particular diet — all in the hopes that he can live to be 150 years old, and that by that time, science will have figured out how to help him live forever."

"Who would want to do that?" Mallory asked. "What makes life interesting is that, at some point, it come to a stop! It has a beginning and a middle, but also an end!"

"I agree with you completely," Dr. Haldorrson said. "I think this whole transhumanist movement is very ill-considered, as well as dangerous, but it's certainly very popular — or perhaps I should say trendy — at the moment. Because of doctor-patient confidentiality, I'm really not supposed to tell anyone what this patient came to see me about, but if you're going to investigate him, I have to. What I'm hoping is that you can figure out who he is, without my having to actually tell you his name."

"Please do," said Mrs. Haldorrson. "Unless my husband does what he wants, he's threatened to make big trouble. In fact, he's threatened to first ruin his public reputation, then sue him for malpractice. Even just suing a doctor for malpractice can make his insurance company drop him these days. And if a doctor has no malpractice insurance, he can't practice medicine. His life as a doctor is over."

"That's true, I'm afraid," said Dr. Haldorrson, shaking his head wearily. "And not only is Drav — this man — famous and rich, he also has political ambitions. He and his Institute have become so well-known that earlier this spring he ran against Senator Jack Hayden in the party primary and he almost won, simply on the basis of name recognition. He lost by fewer than five thousand votes."

Bob noticed that Jupiter suddenly sat up straighter and seemed to be listening more intently. So was he, because although he had no idea whether or not the man he was thinking about had bought the Orion Rigsby estate, he'd heard of The Institute for Eternal Consciousness and that it had been founded by a man named Draven Chandler. He knew that Chandler had run against Jack Hayden in the party primary.

"Now, with the sudden death of Hayden, I think this man — "

"Draven Chandler?" Bob asked.

"Yes, Draven Chandler," Dr. Haldorrson said, "will almost certainly try to take Hayden's place on the November ballot. I don't really care much for politics, but since the man has more or less threatened to do what he can to ruin my life if I don't replace his hips, I'd like to stop him before he gets to Washington. He's already drunk on power."

"And you can't convince him to find a less scrupulous orthopedic surgeon?" Mallory said. "I'm sure there are other good ones."

"This is a man who's accustomed to getting what he wants," Dr. Haldorrson said. "It's no longer even about the hip replacements. It's about punishing me for defying him. The simple fact is that, in all my years, I've never run across anyone who struck me as so lacking a moral compass of any kind. And this is a man who is on the record as having his sights on the Presidency of the United States.

"If he were to get Hayden's spot on the ballot and win in November, he'd be one step closer to that goal. And there's no time like the present to stop him. Do you think the four of you could conduct some sort of background investigation of the man to see if he has any secrets that he doesn't want made public, that might bring him down?"

After the last two cases, in which first his father's and then Pete's aunt and uncle's reputations had been under siege, Bob knew this was a case they had to take. Jupiter looked from one of them to the next, searching for their agreement before saying anything to Dr. Haldorrson. Bob smiled just a bit and nodded his head to indicate that he was in.

"We'll do everything we can to help," said Jupiter. "But I do have a few questions."

"Absolutely," Dr. Haldorrson said. "Ask away."

To Bob's surprise, Jupiter said, "As someone who works at Oceanview Hospital, are you aware that Senator Hayden was supposedly treated for a foot injury there about a week ago?"

Though Jupiter had told him and the others about this before they'd come, he hadn't really told them why.

Dr. Haldorrson nodded. "I actually saw Jack Hayden in a wheelchair at the hospital on his way to having his foot checked. I know him a bit because I replaced one of his hips about ten years ago, not long after we moved to California. And I saw him again after he left Barney Granger's suite. Dr. Granger's a noted foot surgeon and orthopedist. He sent Hayden home in a walking cast."

"I saw him on the news," Jupiter said. "That boot must be very heavy."

"I would assume so," Dr. Haldorrson said. "When I saw Jack as he was leaving, he seemed a little off to me, a little bit out of it. Didn't seem to recognize me. Maybe it was the shock. I didn't want to remind him who I was. But he had an aide with him, a man, very eager, bristling with nervous energy, in his early 40s I'd think. He wanted to know how to get to the offices of a different doctor, a Dr. Avery Eden.

"Well, it's a big hospital, and I know the orthopedists mostly. I told him I couldn't help him and he should ask at reception. I'd never heard of this Avery Eden. But I remembered her name because it's almost as unusual as Draven Chandler."

Or Septimus Halfpenny, Bob thought.

Jupiter nodded. Had he heard of the woman? Bob wondered. He doubted it. But Jupiter was being inscrutable at the moment. "Back to this Draven Chandler person," he said. "Does he have any quirks, or oddities, or anything that struck you as peculiar or unusual?"

"Other than wanting two artificial hips when he doesn't need them?" Dr. Haldorrson said. "Well, he told me that surgery fascinated him, and that he had no qualms about the sight of blood. He claimed to have a surgeon's iron stomach. At least that's what he said, and I have no reason to doubt him. He also mentioned that when he was a child – or perhaps a teenager – he lived in a commune near the Mexican border. A commune his parents had founded, and where he learned that nothing ever truly died – and that after death, you moved on to live among the gods."

"What gods, exactly?" Pete asked.

"I have no idea," said Dr. Haldorrson. "But he said his childhood played an important role in turning him into a transhumanist. That's all I can tell you, really."

It was clear to Bob that Dr. Haldorrson had already said more than he wished he had, but he still looked very grateful to The Three Investigators for having come to talk to him.

As Jupiter stood – a signal to the others that they were about to leave – Dr. Haldorrson said, "So you think you can do something to help me?"

"We can promise our very best efforts," Jupiter said.

"The Three Investigators have solved every case they've taken on, Father," Freya said.

"Yes, my dear," her father said, smiling

at her affectionately. "So you have told me."

Freya blushed, almost as alarmingly as Pete. Bob thought it was charming.

"Thank you so much for coming," Mrs. Haldorrson said as she and her husband walked them to the door. "And for figuring out who my husband's patient is!"

Freya had somehow managed to maneuver herself next to Bob. When her mother spoke, she smiled at him, and he smiled back. There would never be a better chance.

Outside, he walked more slowly as Pete, Jupiter, and Mallory headed for the Salvage Yard truck.

"I'm sorry about your father," he said. "But I'm sure we can help. I've got a lot of sympathy for him. My dad was just threatened in a similar way – well, not that similar, but he was threatened – and it all came out O.K. So you should feel very optimistic."

"I do!" Freya said. "If there's any way I can help, please let me know – "

"We will," Bob said. "I promise."

He paused and took a breath to give himself courage and tried to sound as nonchalant as possible. "By the way, I don't know if you heard, but our friends Connor O'Malley and Charlotte Mitchell are getting married next week, up in Ojai."

"Yes," Freya said. "Leif mentioned it. That's wonderful. I heard Pete fixed them up."

"Yes," Bob said. "He's got the knack. Anyway – "

Freya looked at him expectantly.

"I was – I was wondering if you'd like to go with me," Bob said.

"To the wedding?" Freya's voice was high and squeaky.

"Yeah," Bob said. "Just for the day. Up in Ojai."

The smile on Freya's face was like nothing Bob had ever seen before. Her red cheeks glowed. He almost thought she might kiss him because she couldn't get the words out. But finally she just put her palms on her cheeks.

"I'd love to," she said.

Bob's heart was hammering in his chest. He felt almost giddy. "Good," he said. "Then it's a date. I mean, like a date on the calendar." He glanced at the truck. Magnus had started the engine, and Pete, Jupiter, and Mallory were all staring at him. "Listen, I have to go," he said.

"You'll call me with the details?" Freya asked.

"Sure," Bob said. "Tonight."

"Great," Freya said. "I'll talk to you then."

As he hurried to the truck, a spring in his step, Bob felt great — so great he decided he'd even make Jupiter push over and sit in the middle for once. He, Bob Andrews, had a date. As for The Three Investigators, *they* had a case — and he hoped that he and Pete and Jupiter and Mallory could help Dr. Haldorsson get out from under the thumb of the dreadful Draven Chandler in record time!

4

Septimus Halfpenny

When the alarm in his bedroom went off the next morning, Jupiter woke with a start. He'd wanted to make sure he was up early because this morning his father's old friend Septimus Halfpenny was coming to visit him at the Salvage Yard.

When he and the others had gotten back to Headquarters after their visit with the Haldorrsons the previous day, Jupiter had been almost astounded to find an e-mail waiting for him from his father's old friend. The local Rocky Beach mails had worked perfectly, just as the postmistress had promised Uncle Titus they would. The letter Jupiter had dropped into the postal box the morning before had been delivered to Septimus Halfpenny's house within six hours, and when he'd gotten it and read it, he'd gone to The Three Investigators' website and discovered the somewhat obscure page where their individual e-mails were listed.

Jupiter had been genuinely elated that Septimus Halfpenny had taken the time to locate his personal e-mail address, but even more elated by the contents of the letter – which asked if he could come by the Salvage Yard first thing the next morning to meet Jupiter and to talk with him.

Just him.

He hadn't mentioned the others, and since both Bob and Pete already had plans for the morning, and Mallory was going to work in the shed where she'd found both the letter and morrión, Jupiter would be meeting him alone. At least for a while.

This development excited him but also made him nervous. As he thought about meeting this stranger, he realized what a buffer and safeguard his three friends were in most social situations. Today they would be missing, and while Jupiter thought that probably was for the best – since he wanted to see if he could develop a separate relationship with this old friend of his father – he was also quite tense. He was normally at ease, but this would be different. It was personal, and somewhat fraught.

He dressed quickly, ate a small breakfast, and made his way not to HQ2 but to HQ1. The old mobile home trailer had become a retreat of sorts for him – a place where he knew he wouldn't be interrupted. It fit him like a second skin – he found it soothing – and besides, their old computer was still there, though they had recently moved their new one to HQ2.

Jupiter still had some time before Septimus Halfpenny arrived, and he wanted to use it to look up Draven Chandler and The Institute for Eternal Consciousness. It was a very catchy title for an organization, but also somewhat sinister, Jupiter thought.

The Institute's website, as he had expected, was lavish and glitzy and very visual — filled with slideshows, slow fades as one image replaced another, testimonials from members, and text studded with highlighted links. As Jupiter read about the history of Orion Rigby's estate, he thought it seemed a very appropriate place for the Institute to have wound up being located.

It was odd indeed, Jupiter thought, that Rigby had made his money in steel — a cold hard metal — and had spent it in pursuit of beliefs that were soft and fuzzy and comforting. He thought for a moment of how seductive the concept of spiritualism was — if he had believed in it, he might have hoped that instead of talking to a living friend of his dead father he could talk to his actual father. But all rigorous analytic thought, and all scientific evidence, had shown that spiritualism was a fraud and a sham.

Because of Rigby's interest in talking with the dead, the buildings he'd brought over from Europe had both been purported to be haunted. It seemed that one was an Italianate mansion from the shores of Lake Como which he had had meticulously dismantled and reassembled in Santa Monica, and which was now the Institute for Eternal Consciousness's main building. The second was smaller and more modest, a French provincial house from the region of Provence and the Cote D'Azur. It too was supposedly haunted, and it was where Draven Chandler now lived.

Jupiter had never seen a ghost. He thought back to The Three Investigators' very first case in which they'd investigated a supposedly haunted castle in a canyon south of Rocky Beach. There had been ghostlike presences of sorts in the castle, and they had induced terror, but on closer examination every single one of them had had a simple physical explanation. So had the green ghost at the heart of a case involving pearls that were supposed to endow the people who ingested them with very long lives.

Still, Jupiter understood why people

wanted to believe in ghosts. They were a touching example of how human beings grappled with loss and they stood against the fact of mortality. He was about to do some research on Draven Chandler himself when the intercom buzzed and he jumped.

"Jupiter," Uncle Titus's ghostly voice said. "Are you there?"

"Yes," Jupiter said. "I hear you."

"I've been having a very nice chat with Septimus Halfpenny," Uncle Titus said, "but I think he's really here to see you. Why don't I send him over to your new Headquarters?"

Jupiter's throat was suddenly very dry. He gulped. "Thanks, Uncle Titus," he said. "I'm on my way."

He jumped to his feet, shut down the computer, and bolted through Easy Three and into the outdoor workshop. Then he slowed himself down – no need to appear too eager – and walked as nonchalantly as he could over to the man who was approaching HQ2.

"Dr. Halfpenny?" he called. The man swiveled toward him, and Jupiter hurried over and offered him his hand. "I'm Jupiter Jones," he said.

"So you are, young man," Septimus Halfpenny said, looking at him keenly, a small smile on his lips. "So you are. Please call me Septimus. It's an awkward name, but it's the only one I have." He took Jupiter's hand in both of his. His grasp was warm and firm, masculine but not overbearing.

Septimus Halfpenny was taller than Jupiter – maybe six-feet-two – and very fit. He was also oddly good-looking. He looked more like a sailor or a tennis player than a college professor – someone whose athleticism was individual and idiosyncratic, and which had resulted in a high degree of health and stamina. He gave the impression of tautness – like a string that, if plucked, would resonate loudly. Clearly he was someone whose penetrating gaze missed nothing and who thought constantly and was fully engaged with the world.

He wore a dark blue cotton pullover with a banded collar, a pair of effortlessly casual gray pants, and sandals with no socks. His salt-and-pepper hair was very curly but cut short. His forehead was wide and generous, and his blue eyes shone with both intelligence and kindness through a pair of gold-rimmed spectacles with matching gold stems.

Septimus Halfpenny leaned forward slightly, as if supporting or encouraging Jupiter.

"The last time I saw you," he said, "you

were just an infant, maybe three months old."

"You saw me?" Jupiter said, taken aback. He'd had no idea that his parents had been in California after he was born, or that Septimus Halfpenny had been to Canada. "I actually know so little about my parents."

"Well, I visited them in Toronto. But only once. I must say I'm delighted to meet you all these years later," Septimus said. "I always meant to look you up, but I lost track of where you'd gotten to. I was in Oxford for many years, and then at Stanford. I haven't been living in southern California long."

Jupiter was amazed at how comfortable he felt with his father's old friend. "When we looked you up on the Internet, we saw that you'd had an address in Palo Alto, but I didn't know you'd taught at Stanford. What did you teach?

"Mathematical physics," Septimus said.

"Mathematical physics? Wow! Why don't we go into Headquarters?" Jupiter suggested.

Septimus nodded. "Lead the way," he said.

Jupiter opened the door and went in. Septimus followed.

"My goodness," he said as he stood in

the doorway and surveyed the room. His eyes went up to the dormer windows and cupola and all around to the four distinct quadrants.

"We just finished it," Jupiter said. "We worked on it all spring."

"It's very impressive," Halfpenny said. "My hat's off to you."

"Not to me. To my colleague Mallory MacLeod," Jupiter said. "She's the one who took an old shed and turned it into what you're seeing now."

"And also the one who found the Spanish morrión with the letter from your father tucked inside it," Septimus said.

"That's right," said Jupiter. "She's working in another shed at the moment, but I want you to meet her later."

"I'll look forward to it," Septimus said. Jupiter took him to the formal reception area and asked if he could get him something to drink. When he said no, he was fine, Jupiter felt self-conscious for the first time until his gaze fell upon the morrión sitting on a low table in the hangout area. He jumped to his feet and retrieved it, along with the letter he'd put inside it, just as Mallory had discovered it.

"Happy birthday," he said, handing it to Septimus Halfpenny. "In his letter, my father says he wishes he'd been able to find you a Maya codex, instead," Jupiter said.

Septimus laughed. "That was a joke between us," he said. "After Diego de Landa ordered the Mayan texts burned, the chances of running across one of them was zero – never mind five hundred years later in a flea market in Toronto."

He shook his head, then continued. "The Maya are sometimes characterized as a savage and bloodthirsty people because of their human sacrifices. But their cosmology was all of a piece, and they had astonishing minds," he said.

"Ever since I examined the four remaining codices and the proof they provided that the Maya understood the concept of explicit zero, I've been fascinated by them. I did my dissertation on explicit zero," he went on. "It enabled the Maya to establish a numerical system and to accomplish great mathematical feats – which in turn allowed them to become the astonishing astronomers they were."

"Your dissertation was about explicit zero?" Jupiter asked. "I'm not sure I've ever heard that properly explained."

Septimus laughed. "It can be hard to explain, actually. The world is so stuffed with things that the concept of nothingness can be hard to grasp. If the universe itself began with the Big Bang, try to imagine what there was before it." Jupiter tried and came up empty.

"See?" Septimus said. "The mind boggles. As far as we know, the first time the concept of explicit zero was used in computation was in Mesopotamia about five thousand years ago. But the Maya invented it independently about three thousand years later. With it they were able to become the complex and sophisticated culture they were. They had some very peculiar superstitions and some very cruel practices, but they were also seekers after scientific truth. I've always admired them for that."

Halfpenny put the helmet aside and opened and read the letter. His face looked very thoughtful. When he had finished, he closed his eyes and sighed.

Then he picked up the morrión and examined it, turning it in his hands with an expert's dexterity.

"It's definitely authentic," he said. "Your father had a good eye. Almost five hundred years old, I'd say." He handed it to Jupiter who took it and looked at him questioningly.

"I'd like you to have it," Septimus Halfpenny said. "It would make me happy.

You see, I already have a morrión like it in my collection, and it just seems right that it should stay with the son of the man who found it at a Toronto flea market all those years ago."

"Thank you," Jupiter said. He felt unexpectedly touched and grateful. "I don't have many things of my father's."

"Then you should have this one," Septimus said. "Though it was only his for a short time. I dare say he'd be very proud of you. This detective firm of yours is quite something. After I got your letter yesterday, I went to your website and spent some very pleasurable time acquainting myself with your exploits. That's how I found your e-mail address, of course."

"Thanks for writing so quickly," Jupiter said. "I was hoping to hear from you, but I had no idea I'd see you so soon."

"I read almost all of your friend Bob Andrews's reports about the cases you've solved. Very impressive," Septimus said. "And this Headquarters of yours is really something."

"As I said, our Special Consultant, Mallory MacLeod, actually designed it," Jupiter said. "She's interested in architecture, so when she found your house online, she researched Fowler's Octagons."

"Lord Blackwood's Fowler's Octagon is

quite stunning," Septimus said. "A very comforting place to move to after I lost my job at Stanford."

"You lost your job there?" Jupiter asked, surprised. "But wouldn't you have had lifetime tenure?"

"I did," said Septimus. "But administrators don't seem to care about niceties like that much any more. One day when I was lecturing, I offended a few of my students by remarking that most of history's greatest inventors and intellectual innovators had been eccentric men – men who tended to view other human beings abstractly, as mere variables in a mathematical system. Someone took a clandestine video on a smartphone and posted it online. The video went viral, and the uproar was immediate and intense."

Somehow, Septimus was able to smile wryly as he said this, but Jupiter was shocked to his core. Septimus had simply stated a fact. There was no question that most of history's greatest inventors and innovators *had* been men. Whether they were eccentric and thought of their fellows as numbers was a matter of conjecture, but the other statement was not open to dispute.

In what felt like an awkward and rather

fumbling way, Jupiter said this.

"I agree with you," Septimus said. "Of course. And I went on to say that both scientific and social science research showed that, in the aggregate, men tended to act like warriors, focused on winning and proving their points in arguments, while women tended to act like nurturers, more empathetic and placing far greater emphasis on peoples' feelings. This is hardly true of all men and all women, and of course there are many variables, but over large populations and over time, these generalizations tend to be true."

Jupiter nodded, still astounded that this old friend of his father's had been fired for stating a plain and simple truth.

"That makes sense," he said, "though even among my friends I can see how those aren't hard and fast rules."

"No, they aren't," Septimus said. "But it does make sense that men would tend to be the inventors and innovators. To care too much about other peoples' feelings would get in the way. You'd need enormous self-confidence, because so many would question you, and you'd almost certainly offend those who were invested in the status quo − people wedded to the old ideas or the old inventions. Think of your recent case concerning Galileo, which your friend Bob dramatized so well."

"Yes," Jupiter said. "The Catholic Church demanded that he say he'd been wrong when he observed that the earth moved around the sun."

"And they put him under house arrest for the remainder of his life," Septimus said, "for stating what we now know to be the irrefutable truth. So you see, times haven't changed all that much. My biggest mistake at Stanford was trying to defend myself by saying that feelings had no business in academia – that intellectuals should concern themselves with the pursuit of truth, no matter where it led – which was often to places that were offensive to many. Truth should regularly make us uncomfortable – or worse. Until the Enlightenment, truth was an outcast in most human cultures, and from what I can see, in the world as it is today, it's becoming an outcast again."

Jupiter was afraid he was right about that – though he would have preferred not to believe it himself. And he couldn't help but remember that just the other morning he'd been thinking that if he could have chosen a parent to be part of his life as he grew from childhood to adulthood, it would have been someone like

Septimus who shared with him a dedication to the truth.

Septimus paused and looked around him at HQ2 again.

"Anyway, what I said that day in class wasn't the only problem," he added. "A student who was part of a class I'd invited to my house accused me of being an imperialist and an apologist for genocide because I owned relics from the time of the conquistadors."

"But that's ridiculous!" Jupiter said. "My father's letter makes it clear that your real interest in the Spanish conquest started with the Maya and their astronomical and mathematical discoveries. Surely written evidence that dates back fifteen years, to a time when you had just started collecting, would set the record straight."

"It might, at that," said Septimus. "But after all that's happened, I don't actually want my job back. Not at Stanford, and maybe nowhere else. I quite liked teaching and getting to know young people, but though I was good at it, I've long wanted to take some time off to explore a totally new field of study. New to me, but not of course to humankind. It's the oldest one there is, as a matter of fact."

Jupiter was impressed by the man's demeanor. There was no self-pity in his reflections, and his expression was good-humored, if ironic.

"What's that?" Jupiter asked.

"Philosophy," Septimus said. "The study of the fundamental questions that have fascinated people since they first had language with which to think. Something so inexact and amorphous may seem like an odd choice for a man who's spent his whole life working in the quantitative fields of mathematics and physics. But I find I love it. I want to study it, and get good at it, and maybe even *do* it."

This struck Jupiter as remarkable. Just recently he himself had been wondering whether science or philosophy lay in his future. He was about to say something about his own dilemma when Septimus went on.

"At Stanford I taught a pretty popular course called 'Quarks and Thoughts'," he said. "You see, there's a relatively new scientific theory that the entire universe may be conscious, down to its very smallest particles. Not that rocks are alive, of course, but that the particles of which they're composed have an elemental sort of consciousness. Because the theory melds physics and philosophy, I needed to read quite a bit of philosophy in order to teach it. My current project is to read the ancient Greeks."

The concept Septimus had just described fascinated Jupiter, and he was just about to ask a question about it when the front door of HQ2 opened and Pete and Bob came in. His friends seemed instantly to know who the stranger was with whom Jupiter was talking, and they came over to where he and Septimus were sitting.

Jupiter stood up, as did Septimus. "These are my friends Pete Crenshaw and Bob Andrews — the other two of the original Three Investigators," Jupiter said. "Pete and Bob, I'd like you to meet my father's friend Septimus Halfpenny."

"And Jupiter's friend as well," Septimus said, cordially shaking hands. "I've read up on you guys, so you're no strangers."

Though Jupiter was generally indifferent to whether people liked one another, he found he badly wanted Septimus to like his friends, and for them to like Septimus. He filled them in as quickly and concisely as possible about the job Septimus had had and lost at Stanford, and as he scanned their faces and their bodies for signs, he was relieved to see that both Bob and Pete looked relaxed, comfortable, at ease, and deeply sympathetic.

"It was great of you to get back to Jupe so fast," Pete said, "We were hoping you would."

"I seem to have been waiting to hear from him," Septimus said. "I last saw him fifteen years ago, I think, when he looked very different then he does now. You two wouldn't know, but I'm amazed at how much Jupiter looks and sounds and even acts like his father."

"Really?" Pete said.

"Indeed," Septimus said. "The hand gestures are uncanny, and if I closed my eyes, I'd swear it was Claudius speaking."

The fact that Septimus was saying this to Pete and Bob meant more to Jupiter than if he'd merely said it to him before they arrived. This public declaration of a familial resemblance suggested that this was not a mere pleasantry but the truth.

"I have a daughter about your age," Septimus said. "She's a bit of a nerdy math whiz who does tai chi in her spare time. Catarina. My ex-wife was Italian. Cat lives with her in Palo Alto, and I used to see her all the time, but since I've moved south, it's been harder. I very much hope I can be a small part of Jupiter's life from now on."

Bob and Pete were staring at Septimus,

huge smiles on their faces. Jupiter felt it was incumbent upon him to say something, but he was so overwhelmed he could think of nothing to say. What he was thinking was that, although Septimus Halfpenny clearly liked both Pete and Bob, he hadn't mentioned being a part of their lives or the lives of The Three Investigators.

Just Jupiter's.

Which had been his fervent secret hope.

"Your daughter does tai chi?" he asked. "Is that a martial art?"

"Surprisingly, yes," said Septimus. "It's mostly for self-defense and in the west is slow, fluid, and graceful. But the true masters are lightning quick. Cat loves it. But enough about me," Septimus added. "Tell me all about the three of you. How did you get together?"

"We've been best friends since kindergarten," Pete said. "We're all young for our grade and we just sort of started hanging out."

"Old friends are the best, aren't they?" Septimus said. Something in his voice suggested that he still missed Jupiter's father. "And are you all working on a new case now?"

"As a matter of fact, we are," Jupiter said. "We just got a new case yesterday."

"Something interesting, I hope," Septimus said.

"I think so," Jupiter said. "It involves the father of two carpenters who work in the Salvage Yard – an orthopedic surgeon who's being threatened by a guy who's a so-called transhumanist. Do you know what that is?"

"I do," Septimus said. "The concept raises thorny philosophical questions."

"Like who would actually *want* to live forever," Bob observed.

"Only the very greedy, the very ambitious, or the very power-hungry," Septimus said, shaking his head.

"I'm sure Dr. Haldorrson would agree with you," Jupiter said.

"I don't know if it contravenes your client confidentiality," Septimus said, "but may I ask who the transhumanist is?"

Jupiter didn't even pause to parse the ethics of Septimus's question. "His name is Draven Chandler," he said. "He runs a place called The Institute for Eternal Consciousness near Santa Monica."

An expression of great surprise crossed Septimus Halfpenny's face.

"The Institute for Eternal Consciousness?" he said. "Why, I'm giving a lecture there tomorrow night!"

Good Lord, Jupiter thought. This meeting with Septimus Halfpenny was becoming almost eerie!

It seemed that Pete thought so too.

"Whoa!" he said. "You know Draven Chandler?"

5

The Food Of The Gods

Even as he said this, Pete was shocked that Jupiter had been so forthcoming so quickly. He'd just ignored his own often-repeated advice to divulge as little information as possible when they were investigating a case. But then he reconsidered. The man was Jupiter's father's friend, and Pete could see from the way that Jupiter was acting that he already considered Septimus Halfpenny a member of his family. So he was also a member of The Three Investigators' family.

And Pete was crazy about the guy, who'd exceeded his already high expectations. He'd liked him from the moment he saw him. He was self-confident and self-possessed, really smart and really nice − but one of those adults who never condescended to people Pete's age. Unlike his friends, Pete operated mostly on instinct and intuition, and he reacted quickly to new people he met, deciding right off the bat either that they were great − which is how he felt about most people − or that there was something unsavory about them and they were to be avoided. Septimus Halfpenny was emphatically part of the first group.

And it was somehow both surprising and not at all surprising that this man – who Pete hadn't even known existed until yesterday morning! – had a connection to the guy who was at the center of their new case. They didn't yet know if he knew this Draven Chandler, and if he did, how well he knew him. But the pieces were already fitting together.

The truth was that Pete had had a powerful feeling – ever since Mallory and Jupe had shown him and Bob the conquistador's helmet and the letter from Jupiter's father – that Septimus Halfpenny was going to become an important figure in Jupiter's life. Pete had powerful feelings all the time, and though they were sometimes wrong, they were frequently right. He'd felt, before they'd even met him, that Jupiter would like Septimus Halfpenny, and that through him, he'd be able to do what he hadn't been able to do so far in his life – connect to his dead father.

And that had just been the letter! Of course, Pete had also had a powerful feeling about the conquistador's helmet. When he'd put it on, he'd felt a bristle of electricity. Maybe he was descended from someone who'd actually worn one once. He'd long known his mother was descended from Spaniards who'd landed in California and that his father's family's Mexican bloodlines had almost certainly mixed Spanish and Mayan or Aztec blood.

But Pete had paid more attention to his mother's often-stated and quite kooky belief that he was the reincarnated spirit of one of the Boy Soldiers who had died defending Mexico City's Chapultepec Castle from invading U.S. forces during the Mexican-American War.

Although he'd flirted with the idea, Pete no longer believed in reincarnation, and he was beginning to get the feeling that his mother didn't either. There were too many problems with timing, for one thing – how the soul left the body at death and entered the body of a newborn. Pete had this uncomfortable image of all these souls hovering around delivery rooms, waiting to rush in.

Nevertheless, he had secretly always wondered if he was descended, at least in part, from a conquistador, and whether he should feel proud of that or guilty. But he put that out of his head. There was the case to consider.

"Whoa!" Pete said. "You know Draven Chandler?"

"I didn't say I knew him," Septimus said.

"I said I was lecturing at his Institute. I know very little about either him or the place, but he contacted me about a month ago and asked if I would give a talk at this conference he's holding over the next few days."

"I was just doing some research about Chandler's Institute," Jupiter said, "when my uncle told me that you'd arrived. I'd mostly read about the history of the estate where it's located, and I hadn't gotten to the other stuff."

"Why did he get in touch with you?" Pete asked. "You already said you're not one of these transhumanist people."

Septimus laughed. "Not at all," he said. "Chandler came across some information about a course I used to teach at Stanford, and he thought I might have some insights about consciousness that I could share at his conference."

"Like what?" Pete asked.

"The course was called 'Quarks and Thoughts'," Septimus said. "I was just telling Jupiter about it."

"Yikes!" Pete said. "You'd better know right away, I'm the one who always needs to have things explained."

Septimus laughed again. "Quarks are elementary particles, smaller than atoms. In fact they make up atoms. Everything you can see is made up of quarks, and stuff you can't see, too. And you already know what thoughts are."

"Yes," Pete said. "I've even had a few!"

"In the course, I taught that certain branches of modern physics are beginning to consider the idea that all matter may have an elementary form of consciousness. Not tables and chairs and buildings, but atoms and subatomic particles. And not that these subatomic particles can think or feel, but that they exhibit some very basic kinds of awareness."

He went on talking, right over Pete's head. Pete listened carefully, but it was little use. He was left with the notion that certain particles in the universe acted in specific ways in response to the movement of certain other particles. They seemed to affect one another, and this was very hard to explain unless one group of particles actually knew something about the other group.

Or "knew" something, as Septimus put it.

"So," Septimus went on, "Chandler called me and asked if I'd speak at this multi-day conference. It starts tomorrow. From what I can gather, people from all sorts of fields that have to do with consciousness have been invited to lecture – psychiatrists, psychopharmacologists, philosophers, New Age practitioners, linguists, you name it. Of course, the conference brochure makes it clear that there will be all sorts of lectures and breakout sessions on life extension and transhumanism too."

"Are you going to the conference?" Jupiter asked. "Or are you just giving your lecture?"

"I'm just giving my lecture, Jupiter," Septimus said. "In fact, you'll have to excuse me. I'd love to stay longer, but I have to put the finishing touches on it before tomorrow night. Before I go, however, I'd like to meet Mallory MacLeod, your Special Consultant."

At that, Jupiter sprang up. "She's working in one of the other sheds in the Salvage Yard. Just hang on and I'll go get her."

Septimus leaned back on the sofa as Jupiter ran out.

Pete looked at Bob. "Have you ever seen Jupiter move so quickly?" he asked.

Bob laughed. "Normally, he's not quite so jazzed up," he said.

"I think that's partly because of you," Pete said to Septimus. "He's really glad to meet you."

"And I him," Septimus said. "His father was one of my best friends."

Before Pete could say anything else, the double doors to the outdoor workshop flew open and Mallory and Jupiter appeared, Jupiter breathing hard. He led Mallory toward Septimus, as Septimus stood up.

"This is Mallory MacLeod," Jupiter said. "Mallory, this is Septimus Halfpenny."

They shook hands. "I just learned that you were the mastermind behind this building," Septimus said. "Congratulations. I think it's absolutely terrific. You have quite a feel for architecture."

Mallory looked a little dazed to Pete. She'd been unceremoniously ripped away from the work she was doing and hurried over here by a very pumped-up Jupiter.

"Thanks," she said. "I'm really glad to meet you. You must have a feeling for architecture as well. When I looked up the house you're living in, I was totally amazed. I'd never heard of a Fowler's Octagon before, much less seen one. How did you manage to rent it? What are the rooms like on the inside? Are they all asymmetrical?"

"Not all," Septimus said, laughing. "Only some of the rooms have slanted sides —

the smaller ones. There are four square or rectangular rooms on each floor. I'm leasing the house, not renting it. For the next two years. An old friend of mine from England – "

"Lord Blackwood?" Mallory asked.

"Yes, Tobias Blackwood. Though I call him Toby," said Septimus. "I met him when I was at Oxford. In fact, I dated his sister Winifred and I'm dating her again right now! Though she still lives in England, I'm hoping that may change soon. She spent most of May and June with me in her brother's Octagon House. You'll have to come see it for yourselves. I've turned the whole top floor into my study, and I keep my collection of Spanish and Mayan artifacts on one of the curving walls. I also have another hobby you might be interested to see. Do you four know what a hologram is?"

Pete thought he did, but he wasn't completely sure.

"You mean a three-dimensional photographic image?" Jupiter asked.

"That's right," Septimus said. "It's actually a sort of photograph of the light an object scatters when you shine a laser on it. It's more complicated than that, but you can produce a pretty life-like image – one that appears to be alive. I hired an actor to impersonate my new hero, Socrates, when I made the hologram."

"Your hero is Socrates?" asked Jupiter.

"Yes," said Septimus. "When you come to my house, I'll introduce you. But before that, I hope you'll join me at the Institute for Eternal Consciousness tomorrow evening. I can invite as many guests to the lecture as I want. It ought to be an excellent opportunity for you to observe and investigate this Draven Chandler."

"That would be terrific," Jupiter said. "Do any of the rest of you have plans for to-morrow night?"

Pete shook his head; Bob and Mallory were also free.

"We'll see you tomorrow night then," Jupiter said

The four of them walked out to see Sep-timus off. He was driving a low-slung Toyota Camry, several years old but in excellent condi-tion. It sort of fit him, Pete thought, sporty but practical, and very good-looking. He obviously kept it in great shape.

"This has been quite a morning," Septi-mus said. "I'm glad I got to meet all of you, and especially glad to meet you, Jupiter." He shook his head in mild disbelief. "It really is amazing how much you look and sound and act like your father. You bring him back to me vividly."

He got into the Camry, backed up, and pointed it toward the Salvage Yard gates.

"Until tomorrow night, then," he said. And he was gone.

As they walked back to HQ2, Jupiter calmed down a bit. He no longer seemed so keyed up, but he was clearly feeling great.

"That's quite a break," he said. "The invitation to Draven Chandler's Institute tomorrow night. We have lots of research to do before that, though."

Pete wanted to ask him about Septimus Halfpenny − what he had thought of him, whether anything Pete didn't know about had happened before he and Bob had arrived. But clearly Jupiter didn't want to talk about it − as though it was something he wanted to keep private for the moment − and Pete respected that. So, it seemed, did Bob and Mallory. But when they'd all settled down at the big table, Jupiter told Mallory the whole story − what Septimus had taught at Stanford, and how and why he'd been fired.

Mallory looked totally incredulous. "But that's absurd. How can you fire a teacher for stating the simple truth?”

“Septimus said that until the Enlighten-ment, truth was an outcast in most human cultures, and from what he can see, in the world as it is today, it's becoming an outcast again,” Jupiter told her.

“I hope he’s wrong,” Mallory said.

“I do, too,” Jupiter said.

“Actually, my father used to say something like that,” Mallory said. “But in this case – I mean, *really*! Everyone in the world must know that Gutenberg invented movable type. Morse invented the telegraph and Bell invented the telephone. The Wright brothers invented the airplane and Edison invented just about everything else!”

As they settled down at the big table, Bob and Mallory with their laptops open before them, Jupiter said, “All right. If we're going to help Dr. Haldorrson, let’s get the goods on this Draven Chandler. What can we find out about him?”

The first place they looked was the official biography on the Institute's website. It had been written by someone Chandler had hired and it had been constructed to make him seem like someone with superpowers. It played up the extraordinary nature of Chandler's rise, how he had become an influencer and amassed thousands and then hundreds of thousands of followers; how he had become a leading voice in terms of self-care and self-empowerment; how it had been a natural step from there to transhumanism.

"It's all PR," Bob said. "You really can't trust anything about it."

"What's really weird," Mallory said, "is that it makes it seem as though he was twenty-seven when he was born. The stuff about his childhood and early life is very sketchy."

"Do you think he's hiding something?" Jupiter asked.

"Hard to tell," Bob said. "It says his parents were 'free-thinkers, unconstrained by societal hang-ups and conventions'."

"Translation," Pete said. "They were hippies."

"That's sounds right," Mallory said. "They lived on a commune near the Mexican border, south of Imperial Beach and just north of Baja. It was called The Place of the Light Near the Sea. Chandler's father was the leader."

"Anything about the commune?" Jupiter asked. "What brought its members together?"

"It seems to have had a spiritual focus,"

Bob said, "but maybe one they made up. The biography isn't very clear. It just says they had rituals that revolved around a Sacred Calendar. They believed that life was cyclical, like the Hindus, I guess."

"They believed in reincarnation?" Pete asked.

"It just says that they believed that nothing ever truly died, and that after death, you moved on to live among the gods. Just like Dr. Haldorrson told us," Bob said. "Anyway, it says that all these ideas were important in turning Chandler into a transhumanist."

"That's all very interesting," Jupiter said, "and a little bit disturbing. A sort of mishmash. Is there anything else on the Internet about this Place Near the Sea?"

"The Place of Light Near the Sea," Mallory corrected him. "I just tried to search for it, and all that came up was a reference to something called the Popol Vuh."

"What's that?" Pete asked.

"I'm reading," Mallory said.

There was quiet for a few minutes until she'd absorbed the article. "It's the foundational story of the K'iche' people," Mallory said. "They were a branch of the Maya who lived in the Yucatan Peninsula. It's their sacred text and it tells how the world was made. It was transmitted orally for who knows how long until it was finally written down in K'iche' in about 1550. Then in the 1700s a Spanish monk named Francisco Ximénez translated it into Spanish."

"I found something else about the Maya," Bob said. "They had a Sacred Calendar, too, and they believed that life was cyclical and that nothing ever really died."

Jupiter was on his feet pacing, pinching his bottom lip. "This is quite odd," he said. "Septimus was talking about the scientific side of the Maya. This is their spiritual side. Do you think that this commune could have based its practices on the Maya? That they somehow modernized or adapted Mayan beliefs for their own purposes? I think you two should dig further."

There were a lot of false starts and dead ends, but at last Mallory, through some creative detective work, stumbled on a blog written by someone who had once been a member of the commune.

"She writes that while the commune lasted, which wasn't all that long, it was called The Place of the Food of the Gods," Mallory said. "It looks like someone changed the name

after the place folded. I don't know why the Institute bio uses the changed name."

"I do," Bob said. "If you look it up under the original name, there's a bunch of other
blog posts by so-called child 'survivors.' It looks
like the food of the gods was human blood."

"Yikes!" Pete said. "Human sacrifices,
like the Maya?"

"No," Bob said. "That would have been
murder, wouldn't it? It looks like they down-
graded it to rituals of voluntary bloodletting."

"But not like the Red Cross," Pete said.

"No," Mallory said. "Not at all."

"There's a bunch of blog posts about it,"
Bob said. "They seem to be mostly reminis-
cences. There's nothing thorough or even well-
written. All the blogs are about something else,
really. It looks like the commune was pretty
small and didn't last very long, as Mallory said.
All the posts I'm finding are really carelessly
done, with no real detail. But the people writing
don't seem to remember their childhood with
any fondness."

"I think it would be a very good idea to
track down and interview a few of these people,
if we can find them," Jupiter said. "They would
surely remember the son of the commune's
leader if they were kids together."

But Bob wasn't really listening. "Wait!" he said. "Listen to this! The reason the commune came apart was because Chandler's father died suddenly. It says here that he was out walking on a cliff overlooking the Pacific with his son and his wife, and that he slipped and fell to his death."

"It was an accident?" Jupiter asked.

"What else would it be?" Pete asked. "You think somebody pushed him? My mom is always telling me to get away from the edge, but I just can't help it. You really want to look down."

"We don't know what happened," Jupiter said. "But we'd better try to find out. And as I said, if we can interview some of these grown-ups who were kids at the time – "

"You know?" Pete said. "I was just thinking."

"Danger!" Bob said. "Everybody watch out!"

"Very funny," Pete said. "Remember when Dr. Halfpenny said that Draven Chandler seemed to have no fear of blood? Maybe that's because of all those rituals he went through when he was a kid."

"Good thinking, Second," Jupiter said. "Let's remember that."

6

The Institute Of Eternal Consciousness

"What is this thing you're going to again?" Mallory's mother asked. "I can't seem to keep it straight."

"It's a lecture," Mallory said. "At a place called the Institute for Eternal Consciousness. An old friend of Jupiter's father is giving it."

It was the next afternoon, and after dinner, Worthington would swing by with the others to pick Mallory up and take her to the conference. She lounged on a sofa in the living room of their apartment at the Wessex House, while her mother hunched over a card table she'd set up. She was sketching ideas for costumes for the new movie she was working on.

"Eternal consciousness," her mother said. "That could be dicey, couldn't it? Sometimes I have trouble with just the regular kind."

Mallory laughed. Her mother had been in a better mood lately and was even capable of making a joke. Her mood had improved because of the job and because of the online dating service she'd decided to try. She'd offered to show Mallory how the thing worked, and although Mallory wasn't really all that interested, she'd agreed and was waiting for her mother to finish the sketch she was drawing.

In the meantime, she was thinking about the evening ahead. For once, the event would be pretty straightforward. They were going as themselves, this time – four friends, The Three Investigators and their Special Consultant – at the invitation of the man who was giving the lecture. There'd be no need to act or dissemble. They wouldn't be wearing masks and trying to eavesdrop. They wouldn't be pretending to write a paper for a summer class or to be reporters for their high school paper. It sounded very relaxing.

Relaxing, yes, Mallory thought, though after all, they *would* be pretending one thing. They'd pretend they knew absolutely nothing about Draven Chandler or his Institute. The plan was for them to mix and mingle with the other people there for the lecture, trying to see what they could uncover. Surely they'd run into someone who knew Chandler and could give them some information.

"You and your friends don't usually go to lectures, do you?" her mother asked. "Is this connected to a case you're working on?"

"Maybe," Mallory said. "Besides, it's an

opportunity for us to drum up some business."

"What do you mean?" her mother asked.

"We're going to hand out our business card," Mallory said. "We wanted to do that at the theater festival gala at the beginning of the summer, but we couldn't. But tonight we can."

After all, they'd agreed that there was absolutely no possibility that Draven Chandler would connect them to Dr. Haldorrson or could guess that his two sons worked for Jupiter's aunt and uncle.

"It's not as though you need to drum up much business," her mother said. "Every time I turn around you've got a new case. Here, what do you think of this?" She handed Mallory the drawing she'd been working on.

Mallory stared at it. It was an aqua blue dress with puffy sleeves and a lot of material that puddled on the floor.

"What is it?" she asked.

"Thanks a lot," her mother said. "It's a ball gown. It's supposed to be luxe."

"It's very pretty," Mallory said, glad she'd never have to wear anything like that. "I'm sure it will look beautiful on screen."

Her mother smiled, satisfied. "O.K.," she said. "Now let's get down to business."

Mallory sat up on the couch and her mother opened her laptop and came to sit beside her. Her browser was opened to a site with pictures of happy couples holding tightly to one another – women and men, women and women, men and men. There was text that explained how much it cost and what the basic rules were.

"This is a very demure site," her mother said. "I don't think anything will freak you out. Here's my profile."

She clicked on a link that opened to a picture of her standing outside in front of a nondescript shrubbery, wearing a casual printed sleeveless dress and looking relaxed and tan and attractive. Mallory approved. It emphasized her mother's feminine qualities without making her look like a simp. The profile asked for what Mallory considered to be intrusive details – age, height, weight, education – as well as a description of what her mother liked to do and what she was hoping for in a date. Mallory had helped her write it.

Looking for a self-confident man who knows that the sexes are different but equal. Interested in fun, good conversation, walks on the beach. I am not a cook!

Mallory had tried to talk her mother out of "walks on the beach," but she wouldn't be budged. Still, the statement wasn't totally generic.

At the bottom of the profile were a number of questions. *What was your happiest moment? What do you look back on with regret? What is your greatest hope for the future?*

"So you post your profile," her mother said, "and then you wait to see if anyone is interested. They send messages to the site, so they never get your real e-mail address."

"That's good," Mallory said. "They can't stalk you that way."

"Oh, Mallory," her mother said. "These men don't want to stalk you. They want company!"

O.K., Mallory thought. She'd try her very best to be supportive and interested.

"So," she asked. "Did anyone bite?"

"Yes, indeed," her mother said, quite proud of herself and quite pleased. "I got four invitations for a date tonight. Can you believe it? I really think I have to get my feet wet and say yes to one of them, but they're all so different. I have to write back soon. Will you help me make up my mind?"

"Sure," Mallory said. "I'd love to." She was becoming more interested. If Mallory could get in at this point in the process, maybe her mother would wind up dating someone Mallory liked.

The site had been imaginatively conceived, and the four men who had written were profiled next to one another for easy comparison. Mallory decided she'd try not to make snap judgments but was finding that difficult. The photo of one of the men, the owner of a fried chicken franchise, put her off immediately. He looked beady-eyed and tight-lipped, as though he lacked both generosity and open-mindedness. Plus, he was going bald. Not that he could help that, but nevertheless – .

She looked carefully at the other three. One was a wildlife photographer who had traveled the globe widely. He might have been interesting, but he'd chosen for his photograph a shot of himself posed in a pith helmet and a many-pocketed khaki jacket and elaborate leather boots that came almost to his knees. He looked gussied up and inauthentic. Mallory grimaced.

So it came down to these last two. Both of them were tall, slender, good-looking, dressed appropriately. Both of them were the right age – or what Mallory thought was the right age for her mother – neither younger than her nor too much older. Both had gone to graduate school. Both looked basically sane.

Abbott Johnston was a financial consultant. He spoke several languages, including Danish and French. His hobbies were hang gliding and wine tasting. His boring work life, based on money, was offset by a whiff of danger in his personal life. He looked like he might provide the kind of security that would make Mallory's mother relax.

On the other hand, Gideon Sawyer had other things to recommend him. Mallory liked his smile. He had a shock of reddish-blond hair that fell over his forehead and made him appear younger than he was. He looked like he could tell a good story. He was an engineer of some sort and a self-described rationalist. He sang in an a capella group called The Singing Engineers that specialized in old English and Irish folk songs, ballads, and sea shanties. He sang bass, which meant he had a deep voice. Good. His biggest regret was that part of his childhood had been spent on a commune in southern California – though he was happy to have survived it.

The back of Mallory's neck prickled. How many communes had there been in southern California that people who had spent time there as children talked of having survived?

And if she had now to choose between Gideon Sawyer and Abbott Johnston, could she try not to be self-interested?

No, she could not, she decided. And it was only one date. It would probably turn out to be a different commune altogether, and her mother might actually like this Gideon Sawyer. After all, she needed to be with a scientist and a rationalist like Mallory's father – someone who could balance the flighty and sometimes illogical aspects of her nature.

Besides, if the first date turned into a second one, Mallory would be far more inclined to like the guy if he'd started off their acquaintance by being helpful with a Three Investigators case.

She put her finger on Gideon Sawyer's picture. "This one," she said.

Mallory swiftly summed up her reaction to the other three and then said that she thought Sawyer had an interesting face. "I was having a hard time choosing between the financial consultant and the engineer, but when I read that thing about his childhood on a commune, I decided in favor of him."

"Why on earth?" her mother said.

"To be honest," she said, "the case that Jupiter, Pete, Bob, and I are investigating involves a commune – maybe even the same one, and you have an opportunity to ask the guy all sorts of questions if you go on a date with him."

Mallory's mother laughed. "You want me to be a deputy investigator for a night?"

"Will you?" Mallory asked.

"Oh, all right," her mother said. "And if you're being honest, I will be too. He's the one I would have chosen, all by myself, anyway."

"If it doesn't work out," Mallory said, "you can always try Abbott Johnston."

"You didn't like the wildlife photographer?" her mother asked.

"Spare me," Mallory said.

The conversation had put both of them in an extremely good mood, and they spent the rest of the afternoon and dinner getting along as well as they had in months. Mallory thought her mother had been charming as she'd been given her marching orders about what to ask Gideon Sawyer, and she'd laughed when Mallory told her that she really had to keep at him. When Worthington picked Mallory up, she couldn't wait to tell the gang about the investigator she'd deputized, and how they might have already found someone who'd known Draven Chandler when he was a kid.

They chattered happily all the way to Santa Monica, but they quieted down when they got to the Institute for Eternal Consciousness. A high arrow-tipped wrought-iron fence surrounded the place. Two imposing gates, hung on square stone pillars, had been left open so that traffic could enter unimpeded. To the right of the gates was a large sign with the institute's and Draven Chandler's names illuminated by floodlights.

As they entered the estate, they were stopped by two guards with clipboards. One asked for their names, and after finding them on the guest list, checked them off. Mallory was thrilled when the man said "Guests of Dr. Halfpenny?"

"Yes," Jupiter said.

The other man said, "Here are your badges and programs for the conference." He handed through the window to Worthington four laminated clip-on tags with their names on them under the word GUEST and four expensively produced brochures with the words "We Shall Live Forever! A Conference on the Mechanics, Implications, and Ethics of Transhumanism" embossed on the front.

As they pulled away from the guards, Mallory laughed. "At least Draven Chandler's well organized," she said.

"You can say that again," Pete said. "It's like a military operation."

Mallory thought that was a little harsh. Up ahead, buildings materialized. She could tell they were close to the sea from the tang of salt in the air. The salt and the wind off the ocean had stunted the live oaks lining the drive. As they got closer, Mallory could make out the detailing of the large Italianate mansion where Chandler's institute was housed, its honey-colored stone, its wide corbel-supported eaves, its flat roof surrounded by stone balustrade railings, its bell tower. The sun had almost set, and rows of luminaria flickered like fireflies in the gathering darkness.

Caterers had set up long white linen-clad tables covered with platters of food and tubs of ice and bottles of wine, beer, and alcohol. It looked more like a party than a conference. On the lawn before the mansion a small alcohol-free yoga class was coming to an end, and opposite that, a host of ghostly figures in white moved slowly from one tai chi pose to the next. The landscaping surrounding the mansion was impeccably lush, and expensively dressed people wandered among it, as if in slow motion. To Mallory everything looked languid and New

Age-y and a bit surreal.

A man directing traffic told Worthington where to park, but he said he'd be leaving and picking up his passengers later. Mallory and the others thanked him as they got out of the Flex and clipped their badges to their shirt pockets. Mallory could see that everyone had a badge, though some of them said STAFF and others FACULTY. All were color-coded.

"Where do we start?" Bob asked.

"I'd love to start with the mansion," Mallory said. "It's where the Institute is housed, and, according to the brochure, where Dr. Halfpenny's lecture will be held."

"Let's go," Jupiter said. "Architecture first."

Mallory reminded herself that the place was supposedly haunted and had been disassembled stone by stone from the shores of Lake Como in Italy and then reassembled here, on a small rise. It seemed an almost impossible task. The mansion's ivy-covered façade with its tall ornamented windows was fronted by stone steps that led to an imposing portico with its own balustrade that served also as a balcony for the center rooms on the second floor. The entrance doors were twelve feet high.

The foyer took Mallory's breath away.

Its ceiling rose to the height of the building and, from it, an elaborate crystal chandelier hung on a long chain. Stretching on either side toward closed and distant rooms, the floor was covered with harlequin tile, an alternating pattern of black and white diamonds. On either side a curving stone staircase swept up to the second story and seemed to be suspended in air.

"Here for the lecture?" a young woman with a STAFF badge asked. "Straight ahead, through the double doors."

The doors led to the main ballroom, which had been set up for Dr. Halfpenny's lecture. In the front, a dais held a lectern and microphone. Folding chairs with comfortable upholstered seats had been set up in rows facing the dais.

Mallory was immediately impressed with how sympathetically the room had been updated with the new technology. She guessed that the red velvet curtain on the front wall hid the sound and projection equipment. It was flanked by two doors that led to rooms beyond.

With its polished parquet floor, its tall French doors opening to an outside patio, its ornate gilded moldings, burnished oak paneling, and fancifully painted walls, the room was the height of 18th century splendor. Therefore, Mallory was startled to see three mirrored disco balls hanging from elaborate and evenly spaced plaster rosettes on the ceiling. Or maybe they weren't quite disco balls. The fragments of mirror they were covered with were copper, not silver.

Mallory frowned. That was an incongruous touch, she thought. She wondered who had installed them – Draven Chandler or a previous owner? She studied them, interested to see how they were powered. She saw that, just as with the sound equipment, someone had taken great care not to damage the building. A thin cable, camouflaged to blend into the ceiling and attached by what looked like large staples, ran from one end of the room to the other and draped down the back and front walls. In the front, it disappeared behind the velvet curtain.

"What a room!" Pete said. "I didn't expect to see anything like this in America." Bob and Jupiter said nothing, simply stared around them in amazement.

Mallory walked to the front of the room where the curtain and flanking doors were. She opened one of the doors and saw that it led to another much smaller sitting room. She peeked behind the curtain. It not only concealed the sound and projection systems but also a number of wires and cables and another paneled door.

When she rejoined the boys, she saw that her interest in all things architectural was wearing a little thin. "Sorry," she said.

"That's O.K.," Pete said expansively. "But let's go back outside. There's still time to get something to eat before the lecture starts."

"And we ought to mix and mingle," Jupiter said. "Do all of you have your business cards easily available?"

Mallory patted her pocket, from which her name tag dangled.

The natural light was gone by the time they got back outside, but it had been replaced by indirect spotlights that cast a warm glow over the crowd. More people had arrived – there were a lot of people! Mallory thought – and as they stood in line at the food-and-drinks table, they found themselves chatting with the couple in front of them. The man was dressed in a tuxedo and gave the impression that he had been born in one. His wife wore a low-cut, very expensive gown. Diamonds glittered on her wrist and chest.

"Lovely evening," the man said. "It's so bracing to see young people taking an interest in living longer."

"Actually," Pete said, "we know – "

Jupiter gave him a don't-divulge-information stare that stopped him in his tracks. "In point of fact," Jupiter said, "this is our first visit to the Institute. They seem to be doing some interesting work."

"Yes, indeed," the man said. "You never know how it will pay off."

Mallory gathered that the couple, Barnard and Gloria Helfstiner, liked to think of themselves as major philanthropists. They proudly supported the symphony and the art museum and Draven Chandler's Institute and Save our Wetlands as well as various politicians.

"Such a tragedy," Mrs. Helfstiner said, looking appropriately sad. "We couldn't believe it when Senator Hayden died."

"I know what you mean," Jupiter said. Suddenly he was interested, Mallory saw.

"We were major supporters," Mrs. Helfstiner explained.

"We were actually on a Zoom fund-raising call with Jack the night he died," Mr. Helfstiner said.

"Really?" Mallory said. "That must have been unpleasant."

"Well, he didn't die onscreen," Mrs. Helfstiner said, "though I thought something might be the matter."

"Maybe it was the technology," her husband said. "There was a long lag time between questions to the Senator and his answers."

"You've seen it on the news?" Mrs. Helfstiner said. "Where a foreign correspondent stands there dumbly while the audio reaches him? But this was much longer."

"I don't know what's going to happen now," Barnard Helfstiner said, "though maybe Draven will take Jack's place."

"Draven Chandler?" Bob asked.

"Why, yes," Mr. Helfstiner said. "He almost beat Jack in the primary." By then the line had moved closer to the table and it was time to get something to eat and drink. "It was very nice chatting with you," Mrs. Helfstiner said. "Enjoy the conference!"

Mallory wasn't hungry and neither was Jupiter. The two of them got out of the way as Pete and Bob loaded their small plates with hors d'oeuvres. They were standing to the side, waiting for their friends, when Jupiter's eyebrows went up.

"What?" Mallory asked.

"Isn't that Byron Baxter?" Jupiter asked.

"Who's he?" Mallory asked.

"Look at him," Jupiter said. "You'll recognize him. Top aide to Senator Hayden. They were always photographed together. Hayden couldn't tie his shoelaces without Baxter being there. Very ambitious, I imagine."

"What's he doing here?" Mallory asked.

"Let's ask him," Jupiter said. Abruptly he walked over to Baxter who was standing with an Asian woman who looked to be in her early 30s. Baxter was in his 40s. His dark hair was parted in the middle. He had the sort of middle-aged good looks that Mallory associated with a healthy diet, high quality dental care, and plenty of sunshine. But he had twitchy eyes that darted from here to there, as though he needed to constantly keep track of everything that was going on.

"Excuse me," Jupiter said. Mallory was right behind him. "Are you Byron Baxter?"

Baxter frowned and looked at him. "Do I know you?" he asked.

"No," Jupiter said. "Excuse the intrusion. I just wanted to say how sorry I was to hear about the senator."

Baxter immediately assumed the role of bereaved assistant. "Thank you very much," he said.

"I'm really interested in politics," Jupiter said, "and I can't help but wonder what happens next. Since Draven Chandler almost won the primary in the spring, I was wondering if the party might choose him to replace the senator in the fall election."

Baxter seemed surprised by the question. "That is a possibility," he said. "The state party officials are looking at all the options. Of course, no one can replace Jack Hayden, but we'll have to put someone on the ballot. I'm sure no decision will be made until after the funeral."

"Which is tomorrow," Jupiter said. "Do you know Draven Chandler?"

"I met him during the course of the primary campaign," Baxter said. "But I don't know him at all. By the way, this is Mia Osaka."

"Did you work for the senator too?" Mallory asked.

Mia had long very straight black hair and a gracious smile. "No," she said. "I'm Byron's girlfriend. I work at Oceanview. Oceanview Hospital."

"She's very knowledgeable about life extension technologies," Baxter said. "Which is why we're here tonight. Pardon us." He smiled a bit stiffly, took Mia's arm, and started walking away.

"Interesting," Jupiter said.

Mallory scanned the crowd, looking for Pete and Bob. "Over here!" she yelled, waving, when she saw them. The two of them hurried over. The moment they arrived she saw in the crowd another face she knew.

"Skinny!" she said. Her cousin Skinny Norris, the bane of The Three Investigators' life — and hers — whirled around at the sound of his name. His Adam's apple bobbed in his long thin neck.

"Mally-Wally!" he said. "What are you doing here?"

"I was just about to ask you the same question," Mallory said. "And don't call me that, *ever*."

"I work here," Skinny said. "See?" He pointed exaggeratedly at his name tag. Sure enough, it read E. Skinner Norris. STAFF.

"You work here?" Pete said.

"Is there an echo?" Skinny said, cupping his hand to his ear. "Yes, indeedy. My father pulled some strings and I'll be employed at the Institute in an important capacity until I leave for uni in the fall."

"Uni?" Mallory said, growing increasingly hot under the collar. "What's the matter with you?"

To Mallory's astonishment, Draven Chandler suddenly appeared out of the crowd. Mallory recognized him from his picture on the Institute's website. Jupiter did a double take. Chandler was taut and fit and enigmatically handsome, with a face like a wedge – a wide forehead and a narrow chin – and glittering dark eyes. His hair was brown-blond and slicked back. He looked like he didn't have an ounce of body fat, as though his muscles and bones were right beneath the skin. His face had a stillness that Mallory found disturbing.

"Mr. Chandler!" Skinny said, almost jumping to attention.

Chandler stared at Skinny's name tag. "Why hello, E. Skinner," he said. Mallory chortled. Clearly, Chandler had no idea who Skinny was. "You should be in the ballroom, helping to make sure everything's in order," he added.

"Ah, yes, sir," Skinny said. "I was just going."

"Should I know these people you're with?" Chandler said, in an attempt to be welcoming.

"No," Skinny said. "Nobody knows

them. This is my cousin Mallory and three of her friends. They like to call themselves The Three Investigators. They supposedly solve mysteries."

Mallory was going to offer a retort but stopped herself. As if a cloud had crossed the sun, Chandler's face changed. For an instant he looked dark and a bit furtive, even guilty, though Mallory thought maybe she was just imagining that because she'd wanted to think of him as guilty even before she'd met him.

"Investigators?" Chandler said. "What brings you here tonight?" He was frowning now, as if puzzled.

"Actually, we're friends of Dr. Halfpenny," Jupiter said.

"Oh," said Chandler, as though that didn't explain things to his satisfaction. His demeanor had become distant, even a bit hostile. "What do you investigate?" he asked.

"We investigate anything," Pete said. "It's on our business card."

"Well, perhaps you'll be good enough to give me one," he said. "You never know. I might need your services at some point."

This stopped everyone dead. Pete looked a little sick. Mallory could see that, for the first time in his life, Jupiter was reluctant to hand over a business card. But as calmly as he could, he took one from his wallet and handed it to Chandler. He had no other choice.

"Thank you," Chandler said, glancing at it before putting it into the inside pocket of his suit jacket. "Now, if you'll excuse me." He nodded and moved away toward the mansion.

"Maybe he'll lose his penknife and you can find it," Skinny sneered.

"Get out of here, Skinny," Pete said. "You heard him. You're supposed to be working."

"I'll go when I want to," Skinny said. "No one bosses me around."

"Not even your boss?" Mallory asked.

"Jeez!" Pete said. "Do you think he'll get in touch with us?"

"In your dreams," Skinny said.

"I wouldn't put it past him," Jupiter said.

Mallory watched Draven Chandler walk away. She was staring at him when he paused and looked back over his shoulder at them as if trying to memorize their faces. There was something really chilling about him, Mallory thought.

7

Staying Alive Forever. Or Not.

Bob, too, had a sinking feeling in his stomach as he watched Jupiter give Draven Chandler their business card. It had all their contact information on it, including Bob's cell phone number. He didn't like the idea of picking up his phone and talking to that guy. He'd disliked Chandler right away – though of course he hadn't been disposed to like him in the first place, given that he was planning to hurt Freya's father and the whole Haldorrson family.

And it was really annoying to have Skinny suddenly pop up. It had been a long time, and Bob hadn't missed him. Now he seemed to want to hang around like a piece of gum you'd accidentally stepped on.

"So what are you guys doing here anyway?" Skinny asked. "Is something going on?"

"As Jupiter already told Chandler, the professor who's lecturing tonight invited us," Mallory said. "He's an old friend of Jupiter's father."

"Family connections," Skinny said, nod-

127

ding sagely. "Always a good thing."

"So what have you been up to, Skinny?" Bob asked. "The last time we ran into you in an official capacity you were digging gopher holes in the Napa Valley."

Skinny looked embarrassed to be reminded. Good, Bob thought. "What was it you said to him, Mallory?" he asked.

"Put your hands up where I can see them," Mallory said grimly.

"And then you fell into the hole your friend had dug," Bob said.

"That was last summer," Skinny said dismissively. "This is a whole new ballgame."

"What's your job title?" Pete asked. "Ballboy?"

"Hardly," Skinny said condescendingly. "I'm doing all sorts of important stuff."

"Like what?" Pete persisted.

"I *assist*," Skinny said. "I'm a jack-of-all-trades. I take phone calls. And I file things and I read and sort e-mails that come into the Institute. I have to get them to the right people. Sometimes I write answers."

"You mean you're a secretary," Pete said.

"How much are you being paid?" Bob asked.

"I'm working pro bono," Skinny sniffed. "My family doesn't happen to need the money."

"You mean you're an unpaid intern?" Jupiter asked.

"It's good for my résumé, Dad says. Anyway, it's important stuff," Skinny repeated. The grilling they were giving him was getting uncomfortably hot, and Skinny turned to leave. "Maybe I'll see you chumps later," he said. "But not if I can help it."

Bob watched him go. "You know," he said. "I just had an idea. I hate to say it, but Skinny Norris might come in handy for the first time in his life."

"I was thinking the same thing," Jupiter said. "Skinny at the bottom of the totem pole here might be privy to all sorts of stuff he doesn't even understand. And since he couldn't keep his mouth shut if his life depended on it, any Institute secrets he doesn't know he knows are safe with us. He couldn't be easier to manipulate. If we need any inside information, maybe he can get it for us."

Just then, someone somewhere struck a large Chinese gong. The sound reverberated in the still air. They all understood that the evening program was about to begin. The crowd outside relinquished their plates and glasses and in an orderly fashion began to enter the mansion.

Bob and the others took seats near the front on the left-hand side. He was overwhelmed all over again by the ballroom – by its size and the height of its windows, against which the black night now pressed, by its amazing parquet floor and intricately hand-painted walls. Overhead, the three mirrored balls hung motionless from the ceiling.

What in the world were they doing there? Bob wondered. He noted that the mirrors were copper, not silver, and that the light they reflected was muted and subtle, not like the sharp stabs of white light that disco balls scattered around the rooms where they spun. Perhaps you were supposed to meditate on them, Bob thought. Perhaps they were supposed to help you reflect on eternal consciousness.

There was a scattering of applause as the ballroom lights dimmed and the spotlights on the dais and lectern got brighter. Draven Chandler suddenly appeared from behind the red velvet curtain, followed by Septimus Halfpenny. Septimus was wearing a suit and looked much more professorial than he had the day before. He took a seat on the dais as Chandler crossed to the lectern and tapped his finger on the microphone. Three dull heavy thuds echoed around the room.

"That seems to be working," Chandler said, approvingly. "Thank you all for coming, and welcome to the inaugural event in our conference." He went on to describe what would be happening over the next few days and to tell the audience that tickets were still available for some of the closed workshops.

"I'd like to say that our keynote speaker tonight needs no introduction," Chandler said, "but perhaps he does." A titter crossed the crowd.

Chandler went on to explain that he had first encountered the work of Dr. Septimus Halfpenny because they shared an interest in the ancient Maya. He went on to detail Septimus's education, his teaching appointments, and the awards and honors he'd received. Much of this information was new to Bob, and he was even more impressed with Jupiter's father's friend than he had previously been.

"There may be skeptics among us this evening," Chandler said, "people who doubt that what goes on at the Institute is supported by science. They may think that the concept of eternal consciousness is suspect or unnatural. I think tonight's lecture may change their minds. Ancient religions were rife with the belief that the universe was alive – that spirits animated the physical world. Now some contemporary physicists are suggesting that such beliefs were neither ignorant nor foolish and that all matter in the universe may be conscious!"

He swept his arm backwards in a highly theatrical gesture. "Would you please welcome Dr. Septimus Halfpenny!"

Bob was impressed by the introduction. The public Draven Chandler was affable, smooth, and polished, and he certainly knew how to draw on the audience's emotions. At the sound of his name, Septimus Halfpenny rose to his feet, looking a bit embarrassed at the ovation the introduction had garnered.

"Thank you, thank you very much, Mr. Chandler," he said. "I hope your introduction did not raise the audience's expectations above reasonable levels." The audience laughed appreciatively.

Septimus grasped the sides of the lectern, stared out at the crowd and started talking. His lecture was very polished, and on cue, a large white screen slowly descended from the ceiling and covered the red velvet curtain that hung on the front wall. Septimus picked up a small hand-held device and pushed a button, and the screen was awash in color − a spectacular picture of the Milky Way.

Though Bob got lost at times as Septimus described string theory and cited arguments and observations by fellow philosophers and physicists, the lecture was constantly enlivened by extraordinary photographs of distant stars and nebulae and galaxies and by equally interesting representations and schematics of atoms and subatomic particles.

Septimus Halfpenny was a great lecturer, Bob thought, with an almost preternatural sense of when to bring his audience back to the concrete and literal after a trip to the edge of abstraction. He talked for about forty minutes. When he was done, the audience rose to its feet, applauding. Bob snuck a look at Jupiter, who looked entirely engaged, excited and proud.

"Thank you, Dr. Halfpenny," Draven Chandler said, after retaking the stage. "Those of you who want to continue the conversation may wish to seek Dr. Halfpenny out at the reception that follows. In the meantime, let me introduce Dr. Barbara Hettinger, the Institute's Director of Development, who has a few words to say about what we do here in this grand building."

Dr. Hettinger was a tall, elegant, and quite beautiful woman with dark liquid eyes and long brown hair that she kept gathering off her shoulders and putting behind her. Her goal was to clarify and amplify the idea of immortality. She drew a powerful word picture of the earliest Homo sapiens and their attempts to come to grips with the idea of death.

Ever since those early days, she suggested, the desire to live forever had been the genesis of everything human beings had created – their religions, their music and art, their architecture, their philosophies. She said that the urge toward immortality was an intrinsic part of human nature and the driving force behind civilization.

"In every culture, no matter when it came into being and no matter where, human beings have dreamed, often through their stories of the gods, of a life that never ends," she said.

Though Bob had never given much thought to living forever, and he and his friends had never discussed it, what Dr. Hettinger said made sense to him.

"There are as many myths and stories

about human immortality as there are peoples and cultures," Dr. Hettinger went on. "Through prehistory and history, different cultures have channeled the underlying human desire to never die through their own understandings and impulses. In the Mayan Popol Vu, for example, the gods created human beings out of maize – or corn – after failed attempts at making them out of mud and wood. Thus, the Maya placed maize, their most important food, into the mouths of the dead to aid them in their journey to the afterlife. So it goes." She smiled.

"But in all the hundreds of stories we have told ourselves over the millennia, there are just four basic forms," she said. She went on to classify them.

She said that the first was the story of resurrection, in which death is overcome by the body literally returning to life. Christianity, Judaism, and Islam all believed in resurrection as a central idea, she said.

The second was the story of the soul, in which the essence of a person – an ongoing consciousness – survived the death of the body. This was at the center of Christianity and also important to Buddhism and Hinduism.

The third was the story in which the human being achieved immortality through what he or she left behind – achievements, works of art, fame, and also children.

Finally, Dr. Hettinger pointed out, there was the story of simply staying alive forever. She said that almost every culture had stories of people – heroes or ordinary men or women, wise or foolish -- who had stumbled on the secret of eternal life. She told the story of the Spanish explorer Ponce de Leon and his quest for the Fountain of Youth.

The more Dr. Hettinger talked, the more persuasive Bob found what she was saying. In fact, although he had found Septimus Halfpenny's lecture pretty interesting in the abstract, he found this one emotionally compelling. It had more to do with the sorts of things he himself thought about when he was alone.

"Today," Dr. Hettinger concluded, "all four of these narratives are as present as they have ever been. But for the first time in human history, two of these narratives – the narrative about resurrection and the promise of staying alive are based on scientific research and solid scientific possibilities.

"In fact," she went on, "if you want to live a very long time, and possibly forever, there's never been a better time to be alive. Science is opening up the possibilities that human beings can live to be 150, even 200 years old. In the decades to come, scientists may well be able to find a way to download the human brain into a new or bionic body.

"So, welcome to the conference! In the coming days, you'll be able to learn all about the new possibilities and technologies as well as some exciting new discoveries. If you do not already have them, please pick up your programs and itineraries as you go out. We'll see most of you tomorrow, we hope, at our small group sessions, and then again at tomorrow night's lecture."

There was more applause as the lights came up and the screen on which Septimus's slides had been projected slithered up and disappeared. The reception was being held outside, where the caterers were still set up and the lights had been adjusted.

"Let's go find Septimus," Jupiter said. He led the way, Bob and the others following him. They found him quickly enough at the center of a scrum of people who wanted to shake his hand or ask him questions. They loitered at the edge as, one by one, the crowd got progressively smaller until it was just Septimus, and the four of them went over to greet him.

"Hello!" he said. "I'm so glad you could

come. I saw you sitting out there in the audience and it gave me heart."

"Do you still get scared when you give a lecture?" Pete asked.

"Every time," Septimus said. "Though I'd say more nervous than scared. But you should have seen me on the first day of every semester when I was teaching. After that I calmed down."

"It was great!" Pete said. "I understood almost all of it."

"You made everything very real and easy to understand," Bob said. "It's amazing to think that the subatomic particles that make up the universe may have something like consciousness and conscious intent."

"I agree," said Jupiter. "You gave a great lecture. Very scientific. Not pushing the audience to believe something that wasn't true. I also liked Dr. Hettinger's description of the four basic immortality narratives, but I was quite suspicious of her motives. In the end, she seemed like a classic snake-oil salesman."

Bob wasn't sure he entirely agreed with that. After all, if you wanted to live a very long time, and possibly forever, there probably never *had* been a better time to be alive.

But then Septimus said, "I agree. And I

think the whole question of how long human beings can *actually* live may be answered by human biology. I doubt it will be possible to extend life beyond a certain limit — maybe the limit of 115 or 120 years that biologists now theorize. After all, human beings are evolved animals living in a universe with certain unbendable and unbreakable rules. These are the certain absolute truths that science has been so good at uncovering.

"One of those absolute truths is that consciousness as we experience it is an organic byproduct of the actions of our brains. In other words, it's born of certain chemical and electrical processes that swirl around in the tops of our heads and give us not only the world as we know it, but all the marvels of which our thoughts and dreams are capable."

Pete was really impressed by this.

"So you know a lot about the brain, too?" he asked. "I mean aside from math and stuff?"

"I'm not a biologist," Septimus said, "but I know several, and they all seem to believe that trying to extend any individual consciousness far into the future would result in literal madness. They say that even if the life extension movement were successful at making the body live forever, they've paid no attention to the brain, which hasn't evolved for that possibility."

"Boy," Pete said, "those people at Stanford were idiots. You must have been the best professor."

"Why, thank you, Pete," Septimus said. "That's very kind of you. You've made my night. Now, what about yours? Did you find out anything that might be useful in helping your Dr. Haldorrson?"

"Not really," Jupiter said. "We met Draven Chandler and I found him to be very slippery. But we really have no evidence at all that he's a bad guy, and that's what we're looking for. That's the only way I can think of to protect Dr. Haldorrson from bad-mouthing him. We know he's a self-promoter and a showman, but those are traits he shares with a lot of so-called celebrities. The whole evening, and indeed this whole place, just prove that he's slick and smart and very clever."

Jupiter paused to gather his thoughts and then went on.

"I'm wondering about his political ambitions," he said. "We ran into the late Senator Hayden's top aide and he didn't deny the possibility that Chandler could take Hayden's place on the ballot. But all we really know is that Chandler ran against Hayden in the primary, and that they both saw doctors in the same hospital. Highly circumstantial."

"Oh, Dr. Halfpenny," a slightly drunk woman said, interrupting and thrusting out her hand for Septimus to shake. "Wonderful lecture."

Septimus shook her hand and gave her a fixed smile. When he didn't say anything, she sniffed and walked away.

"Why don't we go somewhere we can really talk," he said, "where we won't be interrupted again?"

He led the way back into the mansion, across the foyer and the ballroom's parquet floor, and through one of the sets of French doors to the stone patio right outside the ballroom. They found a series of filigreed café tables and round-backed metal chairs.

The ballroom and patio were empty by now, except for members of the staff who were cleaning up, straightening chairs and picking up discarded programs. The five of them sat down, looking in the direction of the ocean. Bob couldn't see the Pacific, but he thought he could hear the waves as they broke on the beach.

"It's odd that you should bring up Senator Hayden," Septimus said, "because Draven Chandler brought him up as well."

"Really?" Jupiter said, sitting forward in his chair.

"I'd only spoken to the man on the phone," Septimus said, "until tonight. But when I met him before the lecture, he was all 'hail-fellow-well-met.' He seemed to like me right away − or respect me at least − and he was unguarded in a particular way, as though we could talk confidentially since we were among the small company who, in his opinion, dwelt in the realm of the gods. He talked about immortality, mentioning that I was young enough so that I would surely profit from all the advances in life extension that were coming down the pike. Senator Hayden, on the other hand, he said, had been too old and senile and never would have lived long enough to benefit. Therefore, it was just as well that he died when he did."

Bob was shocked. "He said that?" he asked. "Isn't that pretty callous?"

"That's not all," Septimus said. "He told me that it had become harder and harder to conceal the senator's mental state. He said he was good friends with Hayden's top aide, Byron Baxter, and Baxter had been working overtime to shield the senator, giving him lines through an earpiece, stage managing his live appearances, pre-recording various answers to questions he'd be asked on Zoom calls, and then using a time delay so that Baxter could choose the appropriate one."

Wait a minute, Bob thought. Byron Baxter had said quite clearly that he didn't know Draven Chandler. Which one of them was lying?

"Why did he tell you all this?" Mallory asked.

"I don't really know," Septimus said. "It was reckless of him to say all these things to a perfect stranger, but it demonstrates his arrogance. He seemed to think that he could say anything to me, because he and I were part of some secret club of people who saw the world the same way. By which I mean cynical people who knew the world was divided into the haves and the have nots. I think, in his view, the haves would live forever – waited on by the have nots."

Jupiter was pinching his bottom lip, Bob saw, and was once again deep in thought. "Are there any other indiscretions you can share with us?" he asked.

"I almost don't want to think about this, much less talk about it," Septimus said, "but if Chandler was telling me the truth, then Senator Hayden's death was not as it was reported in the media."

"I saw the news the next morning," Jupiter said. "They reported that Hayden had died of a heart attack the night before."

"But they didn't report that Hayden had actually dropped dead during a fund-raising event he was holding on Zoom."

"What?" Pete said. "He died on camera?"

"No," Septimus said. "It seemed he died during one of Byron Baxter's prerecorded answers, and Baxter managed to wrap up the call as quickly as possible. His handlers wanted his death to be reported as later than it was, so they delayed calling 911. Even so, the medical examiner gave a range of possible times of death that included a time an hour before they wanted him to say it could have occurred."

"What are they trying to cover up?" Jupiter wondered.

"I don't know," Septimus said. "Possibly just that they didn't want anyone to know he'd died during the Zoom call. Draven Chandler seemed to think it was all quite amusing."

"Pardon me," Pete said. "Did you say before that Draven Chandler told you he was friends with Byron Baxter?"

"Yes," Septimus said. "He even told me he hoped that Baxter would support his candidacy on the November ballot."

"Because we met Byron Baxter before your lecture," Pete said. "And he told us he didn't really know Chandler at all."

The expression that crossed Septimus Halfpenny's face was hard for Bob to read. He looked a bit puzzled and a bit angry. A sardonic smile played at the edges of his lips. "Well, well," he said. "That's very interesting."

It was just the sort of thing Jupiter would have said, Bob thought.

Before anyone could say anything else, Bob heard three huge crashes, from the ballroom behind them. It sounded as if a wall had collapsed, or all the windows had been broken at once. His heart leapt in his chest. Something disastrous had happened. The five of them jumped to their feet and rushed through the French doors.

The few people still in the ballroom were all frozen in place. Bob saw to his astonishment that the weight of the three mirrored balls suspended from the ceiling had been too much for the cable that had supported them. The cable had ripped loose from the front wall, where it now snaked up from behind the red velvet curtain, across the entire expanse of the ballroom, to the back wall. All three balls had plummeted to the parquet floor where they lay in shattered ruins. Glass and metal fragments littered the floor. Bob couldn't help but imagine the carnage if this had happened during the earlier lecture.

All but one of the people in the ballroom were some distance from where the balls had fallen, but a lone figure stood quaking near the wreckage. It looked as though he had barely escaped being crushed. He had his back to them but he looked familiar.

"Skinny?" Mallory said.

Skinny Norris whirled to face them. His face was chalk-white and he looked terrified. He'd been in the ballroom helping to clean up, underlining his low status at the Institute; Pete hadn't been wrong to taunt him.

Still, what had happened to him shouldn't have happened to anyone. For the first time in his life, Bob felt genuinely sorry for the pesky geek. After hearing Dr. Hettinger talk about staying alive forever, Bob thought it was totally weird that one of the balls that were supposed to make you think about eternal consciousness might have killed someone when it dropped to the ground and shattered into a thousand pieces. And of all the people it might have been, that someone had proved to be Skinny Norris!

8

The Place Of The Food Of The Gods

"So when do you think you'll get here?" Jupiter asked Mallory the next morning. A breeze blew in through the opened doors that led to the outside workshop and riffled the papers on the desk in HQ2. Mallory had called on the landline to say she'd be late for the meeting that Jupiter had set up for this morning. Bob and Pete were already there in order to help decide what their next step in the case should be.

"That's hard to say," Mallory told him. "My mother got home from her date pretty late last night, and she just got up. I don't want to push her, but I don't want to leave until I find out what she learned about the commune her date lived on when he was a kid."

"Just get here as soon as you can," Jupiter said. After the curious events of the night before, at the Institute For Eternal Consciousness, he was anxious to come up with a plan. When he hung up the phone and rejoined Pete and Bob in their beanbag chairs, they went back to talking about the accident.

"I couldn't believe how scared Skinny was," Pete said. "He was shaking. It was almost like he was a real person."

"I thought he was going to hug Jupiter," Bob said.

"I don't know why you say that," Jupiter retorted. "He was so petrified he could hardly move or talk." The idea of being hugged by Skinny was quite distasteful, no matter what.

"I felt sorry for him," Bob said. "Those balls must have weighed over a hundred pounds each. He was really lucky he wasn't hurt."

"Or killed," Pete said. "He said he jumped out of the way and the thing barely missed his head."

"At least he got a day off from his important work as a gofer," Bob said. "They told him to take it easy today. I suspect he's busy turning the whole thing into a story in which he's the hero."

"They sure didn't want us to call the police," Pete said.

"I can understand that," Jupiter said. "After all, no one was hurt, and the floor wasn't even really damaged."

"Still," Bob said, "someone ought to figure out how that happened."

"I suppose they'll do an internal investigation," Jupiter said, "but a carelessly fastened cable at the Institute really isn't our business. Not at the moment, anyway." He hoped he was right in saying this. After all, if it hadn't been Skinny who had almost died, he might have suspected more than carelessness on the part of someone or other.

"So what are you thinking, Jupe?" Pete asked. "About the case?"

"I'm mostly thinking about the conflicting information we got about Draven Chandler and Byron Baxter," Jupiter said. "Baxter swore he'd just met Chandler casually, but Chandler told Septimus he and Baxter were good friends. So who should we believe?"

"Easy," Bob said. "Baxter didn't know us at all, so why would he tell us the truth, especially if he had something to hide? And Septimus said that Chandler thought he was a member of the gods club, so there'd be no reason for him to lie to *him*. I vote for Chandler."

Jupiter leaned back in his butterfly chair, and after staring at the ceiling for a moment, nodded. "I agree," he said. "In fact, I suspect that Baxter and Chandler have been friends for quite some time. Or at least close partners. I would guess that Chandler's political ambitions

sent him to Baxter months, maybe years ago —
after he sensed Baxter was as ruthlessly ambitious as he is."

"He probably thought Baxter was a
member of his gods club, too," Pete said.

"Exactly," Jupiter said. "One of the people who shape reality for the rest of us."

"But what do you think he wanted from
Baxter?" Bob asked.

"This is all speculation," Jupiter said as
he turned back toward them. "But I'd guess he
was hoping to form an alliance. He has political ambitions, and Baxter is a top-notch political aide. He probably said something about
how Baxter's run with Hayden was close to being over, and if Baxter wanted to continue to
wield the power and influence he had, he'd better team up with Chandler."

"Hitch his wagon to Chandler's star,"
Pete said.

"Yes," Jupiter agreed. "As my aunt
would say."

"Or my mother," Pete said.

Jupiter laughed. "If I really wanted to go
out on a limb," he said, "I'd posit that the reason an unknown like Chandler — unknown in
the political world, that is — almost won against
an old pro like Jack Hayden was because By-

ron Baxter somehow managed to undercut his boss at every turn. Maybe he gave Hayden bad advice or maybe he gave Chandler inside information. Who knows?"

"You mean, maybe Baxter got on board after the primary with the idea that Chandler should replace Hayden – and that they shouldn't necessarily wait until the end of the new senate term," Bob said.

"Yes," Jupiter said. "It's worth considering."

"But there's a logical problem, isn't there?" Bob asked.

"Which is?" Pete asked.

"If Baxter wanted to undercut Hayden, why didn't he just get out of the way and let everyone see that Hayden was suffering from dementia or whatever it was?" Bob asked. "After all, Chandler told Septimus that, ever since the primary, Baxter had been working overtime to hide the senator's mental deficits – stage managing Hayden's appearances and Zoom calls, putting out regular reports about how healthy Hayden was. If he wanted to help Chandler, why didn't he just let the senator look like a doddering old fool?"

"You may have answered your own question," Jupiter mused. "You said that Baxter had been going out of his way 'ever since the primary'. If my hypothesis is right, Baxter and Chandler were both hoping that Chandler would win, after which Baxter could jump ship to the party's new candidate. But when Hayden won, it was important that he keep the seat. If the other party took the seat, both Chandler and Baxter would lose."

"That makes sense," Bob said. "In Chandler's and Baxter's playbook, the time to let everyone know about the mental problems would have been before the primary."

"A miscalculation," Jupiter said. "Still, the primary was extremely close. When Chandler lost, the best outcome for the two of them was what, oddly enough, actually happened – for Hayden to die suddenly. That way, the party – with Baxter presumably pulling strings – could appoint Chandler to run in the general election in Hayden's place."

"If we could prove that Chandler and Baxter put their heads together," Bob said, "it would be all we'd need to make Chandler leave Dr. Haldorrson alone. But how?"

"Hmmm," Jupiter said. "Let me think."

He doubted there were any documents that they could get their hands on that would prove the collaboration. Chandler and Baxter were too smart for that. Likewise, they wouldn't have confided in anyone else. The best thing would be to get Chandler to talk about it, maybe casually. A plan was beginning to form.

That night they were going to Septimus Halfpenny's for dinner so that all of them could see his Octagon House. The previous night had ended with the invitation, and Jupiter was looking forward to getting to know Septimus better, and seeing his house.

"Maybe Septimus could help us," Jupiter said.

"I'm sure he would," Pete said, "but how?"

"Draven Chandler has already been reckless when talking to Septimus," Jupiter said. "So maybe Septimus could get him to say more. He's extremely smart and would know what questions to ask to get Chandler talking. And if we could somehow get Chandler on audio or video, that would do it. Depending on what he said, maybe we couldn't keep him from running for President, but it should be enough for us to do what Dr. Haldorrson asked us to do."

"That's a great idea!" Pete said. "A sting!"

"When and how would we arrange it?"

Bob asked.

"I have no idea," Jupiter said. "We need to talk it over with Septimus."

Just then the front door flew open and Mallory arrived, flushed with both excitement and the speed with which she'd cycled over from the Wessex House. Her eyes were shining as she tried to catch her breath. Her red hair was tangled from her bike helmet and she ran her hands through it to rearrange it.

"Whoa!" Pete said. "Easy does it."

Finally she got a sentence out. "You're not going to believe this, but my ditzy mother *totally* got the goods for us. The guy she went on a date with last night? It turns out he *did* live with his parents on the commune run by Draven Chandler's parents!"

"You're kidding!" Pete said excitedly.

"Not kidding," said Mallory. "My mother really liked the guy, but even so, she took me seriously and remembered to ask him all these questions I wanted her to ask. She just spent a half hour telling me everything he told her last night about what went on at this commune, and how horrible it really was."

"Yikes!" Pete said. "How horrible was it?"

"Tell us everything," Jupiter said. "Don't

leave out a single detail."

As Mallory nodded happily and began talking, Jupiter thought – and not for the first time – how much he admired her intelligence, and her knack for planning, and her straight-forward facility for getting down to business. She'd been an extraordinary asset to The Three Investigators and had contributed something crucial to just about every single case since they'd met her. He was glad that the previous summer had ended with putting her name on The Three Investigators card.

"O.K.," Mallory said, sitting down in the fourth butterfly chair and stretching her legs out. "Here goes. The guy's name is Gideon Sawyer. He's an engineer and a rationalist, but he isn't dorky at all. He's got a great smile. I already like him better than anyone my mom has dated since my father died – and I haven't even met him yet!"

"That's great!" Bob said. "Peace at last at the Wessex House!"

"Anyway," Mallory went on, "my mom likes him too. They've already got a second date planned. They were out really late, just talking, and this morning my mom was in a really good mood. She's been so morose ever since she broke up with that loser costume designer that it was a huge relief. She couldn't stop talking about how funny he was and how much they laughed and how smart he was. I finally had to pin her down and ask questions about what she'd found out about the commune."

"How old was he when he lived there?" Jupiter asked.

"He was seven when his parents moved there and eleven when they left. He said he was there from the very beginning to the very end — four whole years, which he said was a lifetime. He hated it."

"Why did they move there in the first place?" Pete wanted to know.

"His parents had known Draven Chandler's father at UC Berkeley," Mallory said. "They'd all been Comparative Religion majors, and they'd all been interested in the Aztec and the Maya and their blend of science and religion. Just like Septimus. After they all graduated, Gideon's parents got married and had Gideon, and I guess Chandler's father met his mother and then had him, too.

"They stayed good friends, I guess," Mallory added. "And then Draven Chandler's mom inherited a small piece of land with an old farmhouse on the ocean just above Baja. The four of them and their sons moved to the land and set up the commune. They decided they needed something to make them a strong community, so they used aspects of the Mayan religion as the basis for group rituals. It seems the rituals were pretty exotic and involved drugs."

"For the kids?" Pete asked, shocked.

"No," Mallory said. "Just for the adults. And only if they wanted to. But it certainly fit in with all the ideas of a hippie California commune."

"What aspects of the Mayan culture did they use?" Bob asked. "Not human sacrifice, I hope!"

"No," Mallory said laughing. "They didn't go that far. But there was blood. The two families lived in the farmhouse, and when others came to join, they lived in the outbuildings or built their own shelters or slept in tents or yurts. They also built a small version of a Mayan pyramid looking toward the sea."

"Of stone?" Jupiter asked.

"Gideon didn't say, and my mother didn't ask," Mallory said, "but somehow I think not. I don't imagine there were any stonemasons in the commune. Anyway, according to Gideon, Draven Chandler's father was very charismatic – tall and good-looking, with these really intense eyes and hypnotic voice – and he got quite a lot of people to join. This was before the Internet and smart phones and instant fact checking, so there was little way for prospective communers to investigate the guy. Anyway, it was a real commune, and you could live and eat there for free, as long as you made a commitment to give half of whatever you made to the commune."

"So people had jobs elsewhere?" Jupiter asked.

Mallory nodded. "Some of the adults worked off the commune and left their kids with other adults, and some set up shop right there, doing pottery or weaving or whatever and then selling their goods in shops or at fairs or farmers' markets. But the real draw was the rituals. Most of them involved peyote and LSD. I guess those were the major psychedelics. And there was a lot of talk about the gods. There was a Sea God and a Corn God and a Honey God and so on."

"Weird!" Pete said. "Corn dogs I can get behind. Corn gods not so much. Did people really believe that stuff?"

"People will believe just about anything," Mallory said. "Look at the kooky stuff people believe today. There's this other cool detail about one of the rituals. The Maya were the first to discover how to use the cacao bean, and they mixed it with hot peppers and corn-meal to make a really mouth-numbing drink. So the commune had chocolate or chocolate drinks at the communal dinner every night. Gideon said that was one of the only things he liked about the commune. The grownups put peyote in theirs."

"They took drugs every day?" Pete asked, astonished.

"I don't know about that," Mallory said. "But there were a lot of drugs around. Gideon had really vivid memories of having a hot chocolate drink every night before bed, and of his parents and the other adults sitting around dazed or wandering outside. He also remem-bered playing a ball game based on the Mayan game called Pok-a-Tok. The kids had to keep a rubber ball in the air and they couldn't use their hands or feet."

"That's like hacky sack!" Pete said. "Except for the feet."

"Historians say that it was the very first organized game and was invented about 3500 years ago," Mallory said. "So he liked the ball game and the chocolate drinks, but he was less fond of the blood."

"I assume they came up with a ritual that would somehow stand in for human sacrifice?" Jupiter asked.

"That's right," Mallory said. "The Maya believed that they had to placate their gods — who I guess were pretty angry most of the time. Human sacrifice was their way of keeping the moon and the sun in the sky. I don't think the members of the commune believed that, of course, but every Sunday, a quarter of the people who lived there were supposed to give blood at the top of the pyramid — including any children ten or older. That way everyone did it once a month. You remember those blog posts Bob and I found."

"Did he say how much blood?" Bob asked. "I think I'm going to be sick."

"Not all that much," Mallory said. "They'd stand at the top of the pyramid, next to a big copper bowl, and one of the commune's priests would make a small cut in one of the veins in their arm and they'd let the blood drip into the basin along with the blood of the other people. Gideon said he remembers standing and looking up at his parents, and the copper bowl gleaming in the sun."

"Was Draven Chandler's father one of

the priests?" Jupiter asked.

"Yes," Mallory said. "Though I think the men took turns."

"This is so gross," Pete said. "What did they do with the blood?"

"Take a deep breath," Mallory said. "They used it to bake a sacred bread that everyone ate at the next communal dinner."

"Yuck," said Pete.

"Not so fast," Jupiter said. "When Christians take communion, what they're really doing, symbolically, is eating the body and drinking the blood of Jesus. This sort of thing has a long history. It's easy enough to think the Maya were savages while at the same time ignoring the heart of the Christian ritual. It sounds to me like the commune practiced a hybrid – a little Maya, a little Christianity. What's more puzzling is why these rituals appealed to the people who'd fallen under the spell of Chandler Senior. Did your mother learn any more about that from this Gideon Sawyer?"

Enthusiastically, Mallory said, "Lots more! It just goes on and on. There was this fantastically weird custom where they put young children into rock climbing harnesses, then lowered them into a dry well. Supposedly the Maya did this because they believed that wells harbored the voices of the gods and children were both small enough to fit in and supposedly open to the voices in ways that adults just weren't."

"It sounds like child abuse," Bob said.

"Well," Mallory said, "in the commune's defense, the kids had to want to do it, and if they wanted to be pulled up at any time, all they had to do was yell to their parents."

"How long were the kids down there?" Pete asked.

"An hour by the clock," Mallory said. "Long enough for them to get acclimated to the darkness and the enclosure and to open up their senses. When they were hauled up, they were asked if the gods sent any messages. They talked about what they'd seen or heard or thought."

"Did this Gideon do it?" Bob asked.

"Only once," Mallory said, "and not even for an hour. He hated it and called to be pulled up, and he never did it again. But he said that some of the kids really got into it and got all holier-than-thou because they were supposedly communicating with the gods. And guess who one of those kids was."

"Draven Chandler," Jupiter said intently.

"Bingo," Mallory said. "According to

Gideon, he went around proclaiming himself as chosen by the gods and telling all the other kids what he had seen and heard − no doubt embroidering on his previous stories every time. The other kids got pretty sick of it. I guess Draven wasn't all that popular. Plus he had a really violent temper that came out when anyone questioned him or made fun of him. He was always getting enraged and pushing and shoving and punching other kids − especially anyone who teased him about the gods."

"Boy," Pete said. "He sounds like he was a nasty kid."

"According to Gideon, Draven's parents weren't too happy with him," Mallory said, nodding. "His behavior was turning people against the commune. They told him that if he kept acting out, they wouldn't let him go into the well any more. That seemed to calm him down. I guess he liked being lowered into the well more than he liked bragging about it. He got very calm and pompous, but he didn't go on and on about the voices of the gods, and although he still pushed and shoved people, it was only now and then.

"But get this," Mallory said, her voice rising in excitement. "One day he and his parents were taking a walk along the edge of the cliff overlooking the ocean, just the three of them, with no one else around. And Chandler's father fell off. The mother and Draven ran back to the commune screaming and yelling, in a terrible panic, and they organized a rescue party and went back and rappelled down to the rocks at the bottom. But by the time they got there, Chandler's father was dead.

"Well, as you can imagine, everyone in the commune was convinced that Chandler's father wouldn't simply have fallen off the cliff. Gideon told my mother that every single person believed that Chandler had had one of his fits and had suddenly shoved his father while he was standing on the edge, a hundred feet above the sea."

"He killed his own father?" Pete said incredulously. "This just gets worse and worse!"

"No one could prove anything," Mallory said. "The only other people there were Chandler and his mother, and they both swore that the father had just gotten too close to the edge, and the earth had crumbled and down he went. But no one really believed them. After Chandler Senior died, the whole place came apart. Four months later there was no commune any more. Everyone had left and had gone their separate ways."

Jupiter felt an odd thrill.

"So Draven Chandler may be a murderer," he said.

"That's a little harsh, don't you think?" Bob said. "I mean, even if he did shove his dad, he probably didn't want him to die."

"From our experiences in middle school," Jupiter said, "we know that children can be among the cruelest and most violent people on the planet – and their desired outcomes are mostly drawn in primary colors. Surely it wasn't premeditated, but a court of law might still call it murder. If so, Chandler would not just be a murderer, but a patricide."

Just then there was a knock on the front door of HQ2 – three short loud raps. All of them swung to look in that direction.

"Are we expecting anyone?" Jupiter asked.

He looked around at his friends who all shook their heads.

"It can't be your aunt or uncle or Leif or Magnus," Pete said. "They'd walk right in. You want me to get it?"

"Sure," Jupiter said. "Thanks."

As Pete walked to the door, Jupiter wondered who it could be. An old client who wanted a tour of the new headquarters? A new client? Someone they'd recently given their business card to?

The person knocked again, three times, hard.

"I'm coming, I'm coming," Pete said.

He threw open the door and took a step back.

Jupiter looked past him, and saw, framed in the doorway, Draven Chandler himself.

9

A Deadly Clinical Trial

Pete's jaw dropped and he took a step back. He felt the blood rise in his cheeks − perhaps the worst time ever for his blushing to occur. He tried to smile as though he were glad to see the guy, but he was afraid he looked really, really guilty. He had a strange feeling of *déjà vu.* Just a couple of weeks ago, on a different case, Pete had gone to the door of Headquarters and let in a man he had *also* been worried might have overheard something. But that guy had been a hero, not a villain.

"Hello," Draven Chandler said.

He was dressed more casually than he had been the night before, in a pair of expensive-looking jeans and a flashy short-sleeved shirt. His mirrored sunglasses were perched on top of his head.

How long had Draven Chandler been standing on the doorstoop? Pete wondered. Had he been listening before he knocked? Could he have heard what Jupiter had been saying? Pete didn't think so. After all, they'd been talking pretty quietly, and the front door

168

and windows had all been closed. Only the double doors to the outside workshop had been open, and they were far away from where Draven Chandler was now standing.

Still, when this had happened with Kwame Owusu, the only concern was that Kwame might have heard that he himself was in danger. But with Draven Chandler, the possible danger was to Pete and his friends. Pete hoped that the door to HQ2 wasn't getting cursed for him, or anything like that!

"Hi, Mr. Chandler," he said. "What are you doing in Rocky Beach? Are you looking for us? I mean for Three Investigators Headquarters?"

"Yes," Chandler said. "I wasn't sure I had the right place until I saw the sign with *The Three Investigators* over the door. May I come in?"

"Sure," Pete said, getting out of his way.

By now, Jupiter, Mallory, and Bob were on their feet, and Jupiter was joining Pete.

"Mr. Chandler," he said when he was standing next to him. "Good morning. People don't usually just drop in on us, so I hope you'll excuse our surprise."

"Perhaps I should have called first," Chandler said. "Sorry to startle you."

"You didn't startle us," Jupiter said. "It's just that we weren't expecting anyone. Come in."

He beckoned to Bob and Mallory to join them, and then he escorted Draven Chandler to the formal reception area where he sat on one of the comfortable chairs and the others found seats around him.

"This is quite a building," Chandler said, looking around. "I'm impressed. You must be very successful at your investigations."

"We're still pretty young," Jupiter said, "but we've had some success."

Pete wished Jupiter had told him some fib about why they had such a great headquarters and hadn't said they were good at what they did. Wasn't he divulging too much information? *Any* information was too much for this god-talking weirdo!

"I can't stay very long," Chandler said. "The morning session at the Conference is starting soon, and I have to be back at the Institute. But one of my staff told me that you'd been at the site of that unfortunate incident last night in the ballroom, and that you'd been very concerned and suggested calling the police."

"Yes," Jupiter said. "That's correct. It seemed prudent at the time. But your staff talked me out of it."

"Well, I wanted to assure you that I take such things very seriously," Chandler said. "We were lucky that no one was hurt, and no real damage was done. In fact, I've thought for some time that those mirrored balls were relics of an earlier era and should come down. But not quite like that, of course." He smiled ruefully.

Chandler looked very earnest, Pete thought, and very solicitous. He even seemed a bit humbled by what had happened. Either he was a very good actor or he felt bad about the accident. He was handsome enough to be a movie star, and he had charisma as well. But Pete knew two real movie stars, and they had something that Chandler lacked – something solid at the center that you could really relate to. This guy seemed a bit like a remarkable magic trick.

"I quite agree that it's important for us to understand what went wrong," Chandler went on, his voice rising in a bid to obtain their confidence. "So after we cleaned up last night, I called a safety consultant and he came by first thing this morning to do an inspection. He examined the cable that supported those balls, and he found that a bracket that held the cable in place on the front wall had given way and that a chain reaction had occurred. All the fasteners that secured the cable just ripped right out of the walls and ceiling, one after the other. Catastrophic failure, the man said. A totally random event. Couldn't have been prevented."

"That's very interesting," Jupiter said. "Very unfortunate."

Chandler nodded.

"Unfortunate, indeed," he said. "I wanted to come and tell you in person rather than simply call you on the phone. I wanted you to know how seriously I take the whole incident, especially since I heard that the four of you were quite worried about what had almost happened to your friend Mr. Norris." He turned a dazzling smile toward Mallory. "Who, I understand, is your cousin. I wanted to assure all of you that the Institute is a very secure place to work, that we have a remarkable safety record, and that everything is being done just as it should be."

"That's very reassuring," Jupiter said. "But you didn't have to come all the way from Santa Monica to tell us."

"Oh," Chandler said, waving his hand in the air. "No trouble. No trouble at all. My pleasure." He sat forward intently. "And you do know we gave Mr. Norris the day off?"

"Very kind of you," Mallory said. "By the way, are you pleased with the work my cousin is doing?"

Now it was time for Chandler to look surprised. It had been clear from the night before that he didn't know Skinny at all.

"He's doing very well," Chandler said, a bit vaguely. "He's fit right in and made himself useful. But tell me a bit more about yourselves."

He settled back as if he owned the place, looked around Headquarters, scoping it out, and then focused his keen attention on Jupiter.

Wow! Pete thought. He was interested to see what would happen in the realm of divulging information.

Jupiter sat back and spread his arms along the back of the sofa he sat on, the epitome of calm control.

"We're students at Rocky Beach High School," Jupiter said. "We'll be juniors in the fall."

"And what about The Three Investigators?" Chandler asked. "You must be very proud of yourselves."

"Just a club I started when we were a bit younger," Jupiter said offhandedly. "You know.

A boy's thing. Then we got a bit older and invited Mallory to join us."

Good work, Jupe! Pete thought — making it all sound much less serious than it was. The more he considered it, the better it seemed to him that Draven Chandler had gone so far out of his way to check them out. By not being able to ignore them, he'd tipped his hand. He must have something to hide — something he didn't want them to find out!

"What time does the Conference start today?" Bob asked. It was an innocent-seeming question, but Pete could tell it was intended to remind Chandler that he had said he couldn't stay long.

"At eleven," Chandler said. He glanced at his watch. "Well, what do you know? I'd better be leaving." He got to his feet, adjusted his sunglasses on his head, and shook everyone's hand — Pete's last. Pete gripped Chandler's hand firmly, and Chandler squeezed back, hard. So he wasn't a pushover, not by any stretch of the imagination.

They walked him to the door. "Thanks again for coming," Jupiter said. "But you could have just called."

"I'm glad we had this little visit," Chandler said. "I enjoyed speaking with all of you."

"I hope the rest of the conference goes well," Jupiter said.

"Thank you," Chandler said. "So you won't be joining us?"

"I don't think so," Jupiter said. "But you never can tell."

They closed the door behind him and then stood there, in silence, until they heard a car motor start and the sound of wheels on gravel as Chandler left the Salvage Yard. Pete glanced from one to the other of his friends. Everyone seemed a bit stunned by what had just happened. They went back to the hangout area and collapsed into their butterfly and beanbag chairs.

"It's not every day that an obvious villain shows up at Headquarters," Mallory said. "When we met him last night, I thought he looked guilty, but I couldn't be sure. Now I am."

"I'm psyched!" Pete said. "We've already got him on the ropes."

"Let's not be too hasty," Jupiter said. "This may turn out to be trickier than we thought. That visit was intended to put us on notice. We invaded his domain last night, and today he returned the favor."

"I think you're being too cautious," Mallory said. "Draven Chandler is afraid of us. He obviously thinks that we'll find out something if we poke around."

"He was poking around, too," Bob said. "He thinks we may be a threat, but he doesn't know how seriously to take us. He was snooping."

"It was great how you downplayed what we do, Jupe," Pete said. "I mean, it's just a boy's thing."

"Only a club," Mallory said. "With a secret handshake."

"Hey," Pete said. "Nobody taught it to *me*."

Everyone laughed, which relieved the tension, but Pete could see that Jupiter didn't feel as confident as the rest of them did.

"What's he afraid of?" Jupiter asked. "What does he think we might find out?"

"We already talked about that," Pete said. "He's afraid we'll find out about him and Byron Baxter."

"I don't think so," Jupiter said. "It's more than that. If it weren't, he wouldn't have been so careless talking to Septimus."

"It can't be the old rumors about his father's death," Mallory said. "He was just ten or eleven at the time, and though we can all easily believe he *did* shove his father, whatever he's guilty or worried about right now, it's not that."

Jupiter stood up and began pacing. He sighed rather deeply, as if he were trying to fill his lungs with more air.

"What's up, Jupe?" Pete asked. "Why are you so restless?"

"I have the strong feeling that I should be able to figure this out," Jupiter said. "And there's something I haven't fully explained to the three of you."

Pete and the others sat forward eagerly.

"Remember when we were at the Haldorrson's house?" Jupiter said. "I asked Dr. Haldorrson if he knew whether Senator Hayden had actually had a foot injury treated at Oceanview Hospital."

"Yes," Bob said. "I wondered about that. He said that one of his colleagues in orthopedics had sent Hayden home in a walking cast."

Jupiter nodded. "The other day − the morning Mallory found the helmet and letter − I was watching the news when the reports came in about Hayden's death. I remembered that about a week earlier I'd seen coverage of a supposed accident Hayden had while throwing the ball for his dogs. The report was that he'd broken some of the bones in his foot. But about three days later there was coverage of the senator on his way to a fund-raiser, and I noticed he was wearing a regular leather shoe.

"So unless he had, as we say, powers and abilities far beyond those of mortal men, he never broke his foot at all. And if that's the case, then it stands to reason that the whole foot story was a ruse to keep people from asking why he went to the hospital in the first place."

"But what about the walking cast?" Pete asked.

"Wouldn't it be dangerous for this Dr. Granger to supposedly diagnose an injury if there wasn't one?" Mallory asked. "If it came out, it would really damage his reputation. And Dr. Haldorrson seemed to have a lot of respect for the guy."

Jupiter nodded. He was still pacing and had begun pinching his bottom lip. "You're right, of course," he said. "He'd be colluding in a lie." He thought for a minute. "But what if Hayden *had* broken the bones in his foot once. The break would show up on an X-ray, even if it had healed. So let's say that Hayden goes to this Dr. Granger and tells him about the supposed accident, and Granger examines the X-ray and sees the hairline fracture. Then he puts the walking cast on the foot and sends the senator home. Either he really believed there was a break, or, more cynically, he thought the evidence of the X-ray would provide sufficient cover for his diagnosis if anyone came looking for evidence."

"Probably the first one," Mallory said, "if he's who Dr. Haldorrson thinks he is."

"So let's see if we can find out whether Hayden ever hurt his foot before," Jupiter said.

Pete watched as the research team took over. Bob and Mallory went to the big table, sat down, opened their laptops and started typing. It didn't take long at all.

"Here's something," Bob said. "About fifteen years ago, when Hayden was in his sixties, there was a big extended family game of touch football at his estate on Thanksgiving. He ran into one of his cousins trying to intercept a pass and broke his foot."

"The same foot?" Pete asked.

"His right foot," Bob said.

Jupiter nodded. "The same foot."

"I found it too," Mallory said. "Here's a picture of him waving to reporters wearing a cast that covers his whole foot and goes halfway up his leg. It says he had a hairline fracture of the metatarsals and that he'd need to wear the cast for six weeks."

Jupiter smiled. "Same diagnosis," he said. "Same prognosis. Five or six weeks. Yet *this* time there's footage of him wearing a regular shoe a few days later."

"Footage," Pete said. "That's pretty funny, Jupe."

"It's amazing that none of the so-called journalists covering the Senate campaign happened to notice what *you* saw right away," Bob said. "No one asked a single question about the so-called injury!"

"So what was the matter with him?" Mallory asked. "Why did he go to the hospital if it wasn't about his foot? Heart problems he didn't want the public to know about?"

"It's all a guess at this point," Jupiter said. "But we do know that Baxter kept putting out statements that Hayden was in the peak of health."

"If this Dr. Granger is the same guy who treated Hayden fifteen years ago," Bob said, "he could easily have thought that Hayden had broken his foot in the same place. Especially if Hayden said something like, 'Doc, I did it again'."

"That makes sense," Jupiter said. "After

all, the place where the bones healed wouldn't have been as strong as if he'd never broken his foot to begin with. And if Hayden reported the same symptoms as he had fifteen year ago, Dr. Granger might have assumed that the old injury was acting up. So no malpractice."

"Just a piece of evidence that suggests you were totally right in your assumptions," Mallory said.

Pete could see Jupiter looked pleased with the vote of confidence.

"I mean, this is hard to believe," Pete said. "Not a single journalist seems to have wondered whether the trip to the hospital and the senator's death a week later had anything to do with one another. They just swallowed the foot story, hook, line, and sinker. I bet your father would have found out about the old foot injury, Bob, if he'd been covering the senator."

"Thanks, Pete," Bob said. "And I agree with you. He's still a real journalist. One of the few left working for mainstream papers."

"I just remembered something," Jupiter said. "And here's where we dropped the ball. Remember when Dr. Haldorrson mentioned seeing Senator Hayden at the hospital? He said that Hayden seemed out of it, but his aide wanted to know how to find a Dr. Avery

Eden."

"Do you think that was Byron Baxter?" Pete asked.

"Probably," Jupiter said. "But we never did any research on who this Avery Eden is and why Hayden might have wanted to visit her. After all, Granger had already dealt with the foot."

Mallory was busy typing. "Here she is," she said. "I've got the hospital's website up. It says that she oversees all the clinical trials at the hospital. She's the one who's contacted by the doctor or medical group looking to increase enrollment."

"What's a clinical trial?" Pete asked.

"It's where people sign up to be human guinea pigs," Mallory said. "Some pharmaceutical or medical group wants to try a new drug or a new procedure that may or may not help, so they try it on a lot of people and keep track of the results."

"That's right," Jupiter said. "And it makes me wonder. Chandler said that Hayden suffered from dementia. What if he'd just been enrolled in a clinical trial for a drug that supposedly enhanced cognitive function?"

"That's a brilliant guess," Bob said.

"My original thought was in line with

Mallory's — that Hayden was really being treated for a heart problem he wanted to keep secret. But now it strikes me he might have had an unexpected reaction to this trial drug. If indeed he was taking part in such a thing at all."

"But why did he have to go to the hospital?" Pete asked. "Why couldn't he just take the pills at home?"

"I'm presuming this was his first visit," Jupiter said, "and they needed to make sure he was a candidate for the trial. There are lots of reasons people are disqualified."

"Wait a minute," Pete said. "When we met Byron Baxter last night and he introduced his girlfriend, didn't she say she worked at Oceanview Hospital? What was her name?"

"Mia Osaka," Bob said. "And Baxter said she knew a lot about life extension."

"Got her," Mallory said. "She works in Neurology."

"Wow!" Pete said. "So when the aide — who we think was Byron Baxter — was taking the senator from the foot doctor to the department run by this Dr. Eden, he might actually have been taking him to get an experimental drug that his girlfriend gave to Hayden."

"Yes," Jupiter said. "Something like that. An experimental drug that may have killed him."

"This is spooky," Pete said. "All this cloak and dagger stuff. Secret drugs and cover stories."

"I think a lot goes on behind the scenes in politics that we never hear about," Mallory said. "We're only told what they want us to know. Unless something happens that they can't spin."

"You know," Jupiter said. "I'm usually not given to what some people might call conspiracy theories, but maybe we're not thinking big enough."

"What do you mean?" Mallory asked.

"What if Hayden's death wasn't an accident?" Jupiter asked.

"Whoa!" Pete said.

"What if Senator Hayden was taking the drug in perfectly good faith, thinking it would help him with his cognitive function, but instead it killed him. Maybe one of the risks of the drug was sudden death and both Draven Chandler and Byron Baxter knew that. Maybe Baxter encouraged him to take the drug anyway because of its possible upside, but hoped it would have the result it might well have had. That, after all, is what would benefit Chandler and Baxter the most!"

"But would they really have risked that?" Pete asked. "Wouldn't they be scared of being found out?"

"Scared, but also pretty sure they wouldn't be," Mallory said. "I mean, the official cause of death was a heart attack."

"But presumably – or at least *maybe* – caused by this drug," Jupiter said.

"Yes," Mallory said. "But there'd need to be an investigation to prove that. And if my mom's new boyfriend is right, Draven Chandler already got away with murder once, when he was a kid."

"Well, he didn't really get away with it," Pete said, "if everyone at the commune knew about it."

"Got away with it in the sense that no official questions seem to have been asked," Jupiter said. "There was never a formal investigation, and no one at the commune seems to have talked to the police. Chandler would have learned that a lot of things that are actually murders, or that intentionally lead to someone's death, are never prosecuted because they do have a possibly accidental aspect and it's not worth the trouble of trying to bring the case to trial."

"So you think the fact that Chandler got

away with it once makes him believe that he can get away with it again?" Pete asked Jupiter.

"Precisely," Jupiter said. "I've read that the first murder is always the hardest – that the fear and guilt are the worst – but that if a murderer gets away with that one, the ones that follow get easier and easier. Less compunction, more of a feeling of invincibility."

"That's frightening," Bob said.

"Yes, it is," Jupiter said. "Draven Chandler and Byron Baxter aren't like most of the people we've dealt with in our cases, and we'll need to be very careful. But I'm thinking the same thing I was thinking earlier, before Mallory got here – that our best bet to solve this may indeed be with a sting operation."

"What sting operation?" Mallory asked.

Jupiter looked at her squarely. "I was suggesting that maybe we could somehow get Chandler to confess – and that we could get the confession on audio or video."

"I presume you're not planning on sticking a microphone in his face and asking if he killed Senator Hayden," Mallory said.

Jupiter smiled grimly. "No," he said. "I think there may be a better plan."

"Jupe said that because Chandler

opened up to Septimus the night of his lecture, that maybe Septimus would help us. By asking him questions," Pete explained.

"Which is why it's good that we're going to Septimus's house for dinner tonight," Jupiter said. "We can tell him everything we've discovered and hypothesized and ask him what he thinks. I'm sure he'll have ideas. And I have one of my own, too."

"This is pretty high stakes," Pete said. "Draven Chandler has a lot to lose. Look at how far he's gotten. If this guy wants to be President of the United States and if he's a potential murderer, he's not going to go down easily. He's going to fight!"

It was a sobering thought, but Pete was up for whatever it took. He thought of asking Jupiter what his own idea for getting Draven Chandler was, but he could tell from the look on his face that in *this* case, he didn't plan to part with the information yet.

10

The Man Behind The Curtain

It was getting on toward six o'clock, and Mallory was back in the Wessex House apartment, sitting in the living room with her mother as they waited for Gideon Sawyer to arrive. Mallory couldn't remember a time since they'd come back to Rocky Beach after the death of her father when her mother had seemed so happy.

She also looked lovely, Mallory thought – like her best self. She was wearing a summery light blue and white dress that grazed her kneecaps, and she'd put her hair up in a bun. She'd been very cautious with the makeup and perfume – just a whiff of gardenias and a touch of mascara. She looked younger than she had in two whole years.

"So where's he taking you?" Mallory asked.

"He didn't say," her mother told her. "He just asked me if I liked seafood. And he suggested I bring a sweater."

"Sounds like you're eating on the ocean," Mallory said. "Nice."

"I hope we're not going all the way down to Santa Monica," her mother said, "though if we did, there are lots of nice clubs we could go to afterwards."

"Maybe he'll take you to the Pier," Mallory said.

"You mean the amusement park?" her mother said. "I don't think so. Not on a second date. He doesn't know me that well yet."

Mallory was also waiting to be picked up – Worthington would be arriving shortly, with the gang in tow, to take them to Septimus Halfpenny's house for dinner. Mallory couldn't decide what she was most excited about – meeting this Gideon Sawyer, getting to know Septimus better, or seeing a Fowler's Octagon in person.

"And you're going to dinner where again?" her mother asked.

"Remember I told you the lecturer last night was a friend of Jupiter's father? Well, he's invited us all to his house tonight," Mallory said. "He's really pretty interesting. He taught mathematical physics at both Oxford and Stanford, and then Stanford kicked him out because of something he said off-the-cuff in class."

"What was that?" her mother asked.

"He said that most inventors and innovators over the centuries had been eccentric men who thought about human beings pretty abstractly. That they tended to be guided by cold-blooded analysis rather than emotions."

"Well," Mallory's mother said. "That's true enough, isn't it? Why on earth would they fire him for saying that?"

"I don't know," Mallory said. "I mean, I can easily imagine Dad saying something like that. In fact, I think he probably did."

"One of your father's favorite sayings," her mother told her, "was about truth being an outcast for most of human history but finally being welcomed in modern times."

Mallory remembered hearing her father say that on any number of occasions, but she was amazed to hear her mother quote her father so exactly. There had been times since his death when Mallory suspected her mother had forgotten most of what their life had been like together. She was glad to discover that wasn't so. Perhaps her own grief had kept her from seeing her mother's.

But her mother wasn't finished. In fact, it seemed she had a lot to say on the subject, and Mallory was pleased to see how clear-headed and smart her mother was when she wanted to be.

"Your father would have been horrified at what you just told me," she said. "The world is changing fast these days. Scientists are under pressure to put peoples' emotional needs first. And an incredible number of people are going along, pretending things that just aren't true. Men and women are clearly different. As the French would say, *Vive la différence*. One of the things women have always liked about men is that they're bigger and stronger and tougher than we are. In fact, one of the things I like about Gideon is how traditionally masculine he is. He's tall and he's got a deep voice."

"And muscles, I bet," said Mallory.

Her mother laughed. "Of course I've just met him, and you can judge for yourself when he gets here. He's sure of himself without being at all arrogant; he's got a kind of nice quiet confidence. He told me he was in the Navy for six years after college."

"An officer and a gentleman," Mallory said.

Her mother laughed again. "Now don't make fun. I think you'll like him."

Mallory was impressed. Over the past two years, when she'd poked fun or been sarcastic, her mother had gotten defensive and started to mope or sulk. Gideon Sawyer had had a remarkable effect on her.

"So what kind of engineer is he?" Mallory asked.

"He's a civil engineer, like your father, but he works mostly with historic landmarks. I can't remember the name of the group he belongs to, but it's a society of American engineers, and they've selected a couple of hundred engineering landmarks throughout the world – amazing engineering feats that people doubted could ever be built. And some of the ones they've chosen are right here in California."

"Like what?" Mallory asked.

"You know one of them pretty well," her mother said, "since you said you were on it last summer about a million times on one of your cases – the Bay Bridge between San Francisco and Oakland. The Golden Gate Bridge, too, of course. Also historic railroad bridges and hydroelectric projects like the Hoover Dam – though that's in Nevada. You know the kind of thing."

Mallory did indeed. But more than her mother's recitation of engineering marvels, Mallory was struck by how clearly she remembered their last case of the previous summer. It seemed she'd been paying attention to Mallory's stories about her adventures with The Three Investigators all along.

Just then there was a knock on the apartment door and her mother went to open it — not seeming either flirty or anxious but with a serene composure. She came back with Gideon Sawyer.

"Gideon," she said, "this is my daughter Mallory. Mallory, this is Gideon Sawyer."

"I'm pleased to meet you," Gideon said, shaking her hand.

He looked different from his photograph on the dating site — he was even better looking, taller, and broad-shouldered. He had a pleasingly deep voice. He also had wide cheekbones and a square chiseled clean-shaven chin. His reddish-blond hair was cut short; his eyes were gray; and he gave the impression of power — of someone so easy in his own skin that there was no reason you shouldn't be comfortable in yours. He was effortlessly masculine without being in any way overbearing.

Mallory liked him instantly. Though she'd admitted that the possibility that he'd spent part of his childhood in Draven Chandler's parents' commune had influenced her when she'd encouraged her mother to choose him, she now thought that, regardless of his childhood, he looked like a solid choice for her mother's latest boyfriend.

Up until now, her mother had dated one dud after another, and it suddenly occurred to Mallory that part of the problem had been that the men she'd dated had been too much like her. Her mother was so stereotypically feminine that she needed a masculine man in order to relax and feel comfortable. The men she'd met through her job, including the ghastly costume designer, had been self-effacing and passive, even retiring. Mallory's mother was like a jewel with many facets, and she needed a man, like Mallory's father, who could provide the appropriate setting to show her off – a man who could let her shine. Gideon Sawyer looked like a keeper.

Still, he seemed a little shy with her at first, and Mallory realized that while he was in his element with a woman like her mother, he might not know quite what to do with a girl like Mallory. And of course he worked mostly with other men. She decided to try her best to make him feel comfortable around her.

"I'm pleased to meet you too," she said. "I wondered what the name is of the organization you work for. My mother couldn't remember."

"The American Society of Civil Engineers," Gideon said. "I work in Historic Landmarks."

"My father always told me that the Brooklyn Bridge and the Erie Canal were two of the most amazing American engineering feats of the 19th century," Mallory said.

He looked at her, surprised. "Your father was right," he said. "They're both on the Society's list of two hundred, worldwide."

She could see him start to relax – to understand that she and he might have more in common than it had at first appeared.

"I think there are four or five on the list in Scotland, but the only one I can remember at the moment is the Forth Bridge – the railway bridge over the Firth of Forth," Gideon said.

"I've been on it, and it's amazing," Mallory said. "I took a train across that bridge, with my father. We were on our way to Dumferline. What's the type of construction called?"

"It's a cantilever bridge," Gideon said. "Its main span is the second longest in the world."

Mallory thought she could go on talking to Gideon Sawyer all night, but just then, through the window, she saw the Flex pull up and she hastily got to her feet.

"Sorry I have to rush off," she said, "but my ride just got here. It was great to meet you. Thanks for telling my mother all about that commune you were in. I hope you don't mind that she told me about it."

"Not at all," Gideon said. "Your mother said you and your friends are investigators. Well, good luck to you! That Draven Chandler is a weird one. He invites investigation!"

"Bye, sweetie," her mother said. "Have fun."

"You, too," Mallory said.

As she left, she could see her mother looking at Gideon and Gideon looking at her mother, and she had a wild surge of hope that this guy might turn out to be the one. Still, as she climbed into the car, she tried to shove that out of her mind and focus on the evening ahead.

Everyone was in a good mood, especially Jupiter, as they looked forward to spending more time with Septimus Halfpenny. The Octagon House was about fifteen minutes away, and for most of the trip they talked about how Septimus might be able to help them find out the truth about Draven Chandler. They also talked a little about Winifred Blackwood, the

British woman Septimus was dating — the woman whose brother actually owned the Octagon House. Mallory brought up the subject because she thought Worthington might be interested — and he was. But when he pulled up in front of Halfpenny's house, all any of them could do was gawk.

The Octagon House was set on a plot of about a half-acre, the western border of which was a bluff overlooking the Pacific Ocean. The land was wind-swept and weathered, with stunted live oaks and Monterey cypress. Its closest neighbors were modern, glass-fronted boxes, but Mallory saw only the house before her. The photographs had been impressive, but they were nothing compared to the real thing.

It looked massive, with its three stories and extraordinary domed roof, cupola, and spire. The house was more round than square, and the wide covered porch that surrounded it gave the impression of a carousel. The entire house was painted white, but it looked pinkish in the sun's rays as it began its descent over the water. The house seemed to vibrate as it rose to its gray slate-covered dome. The ranks of paired corbelled columns supporting the porch roof were mirrored by the ranks of tall paired arched windows above it whose glass gleamed golden in the lowering sun. It was a fairy tale house, Mallory thought – something from a dream, but so imposing that it carried a whiff of menace. It commanded the landscape in an almost domineering fashion.

"Yikes!" Pete said. "You sure were right, Mallory. It does look like a head. And it's got a cupola. Like the one on HQ2!"

The cupola on the Octagon House was bigger than the one Mallory had designed for their new Headquarters, but they *were* similar, and Mallory was pleased that Pete had noticed. The four of them got out and had soon walked up the curving steps to the wraparound porch where they waved goodbye to Worthington – who'd said he'd come back when they called him.

Jupiter rang the doorbell, and the four of them stood there expectantly until the tall shadow of Septimus Halfpenny filled the etched glass of one of the double arched entry doors.

"Welcome!" he said, as he swept the door open. "Come in!"

The entry hall alone was bigger than most rooms in most houses, with a globe chandelier hanging from the center of the ten-foot ceiling. The oak floor was highly polished and the walls were decorated with hand-painted gilded friezes.

"Let me give you a quick tour," Septimus said. "Quick, mind you."

Mallory's mind whirled as they walked through the house. Off the entry hall were two rooms – a sunroom looking toward the Pacific and a library. A long hall led to the dining room, which opened onto a pantry, a tearoom, and an expansive and well-stocked kitchen. There was also a large rectangular sitting room, full of comfortable chairs and two sofas.

The stairs off the entry hall led to the second floor where there were four bedrooms and another sitting room. One of the bedrooms was larger and messier than the others, and when she peeked inside it, at Septimus's invitation, Mallory could see that he had recently shared the bedroom with a woman, whose toiletries and clothing were in evidence.

But it was the third floor that truly stunned Mallory. It was a single huge room – a perfect octagon with double arched dormer windows on each of the eight sides. Because of the house's domed roof, the rich paneled walls curved inward, covered by the same wood as the floor, all varnished to a high gloss. There was a rather large cabinet or closet spanning almost the length of one of the eight walls, built

of the same wood, and therefore almost invisible. The room gave Mallory the feeling that
she was inside a luxurious hatbox.

The windows did not curve, of course.
Their dormers jutted out from the roof in all
eight directions. Each of the windows had been
fitted with cunning electrically-operated black-
out shades that, as Septimus demonstrated,
were operated by a single switch. When they
closed, the room was as dark as if it were
night.

But when they were open, there were
far-ranging breathtaking views of the ocean
and the houses to the north and south, the distant winding streets and avenues of Rocky
Beach, a panoramic bird's-eye view of the
whole human world — a bit like God might see
it, Mallory thought, if there *were* a God.

"This is your study?" Bob asked.

"Yes," Septimus said. "The reason I
wanted to lease the house."

He'd divided the room into distinct areas
through the groupings of furniture and the
strategic positioning of freestanding bookcases.
He'd placed a desk, desk chair, easy chair, and
standing lamp to one side. Opposite it, a rather
grand upholstered chair, not unlike a throne,
stood against the wall. It seemed rather odd to

Mallory, sitting there all alone.

On the curving wall between the desk and the upholstered chair, Septimus had exhibited his collection of Spanish and Mayan artifacts, and in the very center of the room, an intricate circular wooden staircase rose to the cupola – which Septimus called the observatory. Though the observatory was much smaller than any other room in the house – perching as it did at the very top – it was eight-sided as well.

In each of its sides, a single window opened onto the slate-covered dome and was fitted with the same type of electrically-controlled shades as the study and operated by a switch down there as well. The top of the circular staircase occupied the center, and around it was an open walkway, about four feet wide. A single antique gaslight hung from the wood-paneled ceiling. At night, Mallory thought, not only would you be able to see the heavens ablaze with stars, but the earth beneath, with its twinkling human lights, would look like a mirror of the heavens.

Though Septimus's easy hospitality had put all four of them at ease, the house still seemed to have struck them speechless. They made appreciative noises as Septimus moved them ever higher, but no one really said anything at all until Pete finally blurted, "Don't you get lonely in this house when Winifred isn't here?"

They were on their way down the spiral staircase to the study when he asked it, and everyone laughed. Pete, as usual, had managed to say what Mallory and the others were only thinking. The house was big enough for a small army; it was hard to fathom living in its myriad rooms by oneself. It was spectacular, and it set Mallory's mind ablaze, but she wouldn't have wanted to live in it.

"It *is* large for one person," Septimus said. "But as I said, I'm hoping that Winnie will join me here soon. And my lease is only for two years. I don't think I've told you this yet, but the reason I'm in the area to begin with is that I've gotten a job with a think tank, and every morning when I wake up here, I'm inspired all over again."

"Can we look at the armor and stuff?" Pete asked.

"Sure," Septimus said. "Go ahead."

Mallory, Pete, Jupiter, and Bob crowded around the collection that Septimus had mounted. Mallory saw the morrión Septimus had told Jupiter he already had, as well as a dented breastplate and an entire set of chain mail. Other helmets, as well – one that was just a dome with a wide flat brim, and another that looked like a steel balaclava that covered the entire face in a cage.

There were weapons, too, wooden spears with iron tips, and flexible steel swords, both short swords and long swords. There were Mayan weapons as well, maces and stone axes. Mallory shuddered to think of the advantage the Europeans had over the indigenous peoples. There were only a few Mayan artifacts – an incense burner and part of a vase. But Septimus had posters of several of the Mayan codices, as well as a transliterated page of the Popol Vuh.

Jupiter was eying the short sword. It lay in brackets attached to the wall. It was about three feet long and double-bladed. He turned to Septimus. "May I take this down?" he asked.

"Jupiter's a fencer," Pete said. "He's really good."

"Well, certainly," Septimus said. "But it's sharp. It's Toledo steel – the very best the Spanish had."

Jupiter gingerly raised it from its brackets and made sure that no one was around him.

He assumed a fencer's pose and then lunged forward and then swished the blade through the air, snick, snick, snick.

"Whoa!" Pete said. "Look out, Mayas."

Jupiter carefully put the blade back in its cradle.

"Now," Septimus said. "For my other hobby."

"Your hologram," Jupiter said. "The one who looks like Socrates and, I imagine, sits in that wooden throne."

"That's right," said Septimus. "I'm amazed you remembered."

"I had a reason to," said Jupiter. "Can we see the hologram in action?"

"Of course," Septimus said. He went to the wall and flicked the switches that closed the shades in the cupola and the study. Mallory watched as the sixteen shades in the windows surrounding her all descended together. When they were shut, the room was totally dark.

"Here goes," said Septimus.

He flicked another switch. There was a brief whirring, and then a ghostly figure materialized, sitting in the throne-like chair opposite Septimus's desk. It was both real and unreal – three-dimensional, yet Mallory was sure that if she walked up to it, she could put her hand right through it. It was the figure of a man with a high open forehead, long curly hair, and a curly mustache and beard, wearing what looked like a sheet draped over one shoulder and gathered around his torso. A toga, Mallory thought.

"Meet Socrates," Septimus said. "Or rather the actor I hired to impersonate him when I made the hologram. Or rather, an image of scattered light. But very convincing, don't you think?"

"Completely. And scary," Pete said.

"Good evening, Socrates," Septimus said, addressing the hologram. "How are you tonight?"

"Why do you ask?" the hologram answered. "Am I not as I always am?" He looked totally lifelike to Mallory, if a bit insubstantial. He appeared to be listening when Septimus spoke, and when he answered, he moved his hands and arms and body just as a man would when he was talking.

"You appear to be so," Septimus said.

"But you do not know for sure?" the hologram asked. "How am I different?" His voice was probing, trying to pin Septimus down.

"You seem a little more restless," Septimus said.

"But why do you assume that?" the hologram asked, sitting back in the throne. He now looked skeptical, wondering what the evidence was that would cause Septimus to come to his conclusion. "How do you know what you presume to know?"

"I use the evidence of my senses," Septimus said.

"But are they infallible?" Socrates asked. "Have they never confused you?"

"You might as well ask me 'What is the nature of truth'?" Septimus said.

"What *is* the nature of truth?" Socrates asked.

Septimus flicked a switch and the hologram froze.

"He and I could go on all night. This is a serious hobby," Septimus said as he flicked some switches. Socrates disappeared and the window shades rose, bathing the room in the fading light of day.

"How did you do that?" Bob asked, mystified.

"As I told you, I made a recording of an actor I hired and then I manipulated it; I'm using AI to experiment with dialogue. There's a projector hidden in the ceiling. It's bracing to engage with a mind like Socrates's."

Which was really his *own* mind, of course, Mallory thought. "What are you studying?" she asked him.

"The subject we arrived at," Septimus said. "The nature of truth. The Greeks were something new in human history. Truth seekers to the bone. And even before that, you had cultures like the Mesopotamians and the Maya that were at least trying to get to the bottom of things. Of course, most human cultures, even after the Enlightenment, have suffered from blind spots. It's funny how hard it can be to see what's right in front of your nose sometimes. And when you finally do see it, it's a lot like pulling back a curtain only to find a door or window behind it."

An unexpected image flooded Mallory's mind – an image from the night before. She'd been curious about the red velvet curtain that covered the wall at the front of the ballroom, and she'd pulled it aside to discover the sound and projection system, as well as the bracket that held the cable that snaked up the wall and across the ceiling and that the three metal disco balls were attached to. And behind that curtain was also an almost invisible door.

A door, she thought suddenly, that

someone might have used to enter the ballroom and leave it — all the while concealed by the curtain and unseen by anyone in the larger room.

Was it possible, she wondered, that the apparent accident of the night before hadn't been an accident at all? Had someone who slipped in through the almost invisible door been standing in the control booth at the time that Skinny was cleaning up? Had that someone seen him standing under one of the balls and swiftly ripped the bracket from the wall, starting the chain reaction that had sent the balls plummeting to the floor?

But why, Mallory wondered, would someone want to murder Skinny?

Sure, he was annoying.

But murder him? She looked at her friends who were talking to Septimus about holograms. A cold hard pebble of fear formed in Mallory's stomach and wouldn't leave her alone. Bob seemed to notice what had happened and looked at her in concern.

11

A Ghost For Draven Chandler

Two hours later, Bob and the others were seated around a long oval mahogany table. Bob had seen the ornate dining room of the Octagon House briefly on the whirlwind tour that Septimus had given them, but he hadn't really thought about how strange it would be to eat in this rectangular room at the very back of the house, its two sets of floor-to-ceiling windows overlooking the wraparound porch and the garden beyond.

It turned out that Septimus didn't cook. He told them that Winifred Blackwood was a terrific cook, but that when he was on his own, he subsisted on a diet of salads, sandwiches, soups, and frozen foods. So he'd decided to have the dinner catered, and the meal had been delivered that afternoon. All Septimus had had to do was warm it up.

"I can turn on an oven," he'd said, "but that's the limit of my kitchen prowess." The dinner was fancier than anything Bob could remember the four of them going to before.

But despite the food, silver, and china,

which might have made them constrained and tense, wary of minding their manners, the mood at dinner had been relaxed and happy. Bob had rarely seen Jupiter so comfortable at what was, after all, a social event. He'd been glad to see him continuing to get along with his father's old friend — as well, if not better, than he had hoped he would.

Bob sat back in his chair, utterly content. It was fun to be treated so well. The crystal water glasses glittered in the dim light the overhead chandelier cast, and the candles that Septimus had lit were reflected in the windows' glass. It was now fully dark outside.

"Are you all full?" Septimus asked. "There's more of everything in the kitchen."

Bob looked at Pete. He had already had seconds, and if any of them were going to take Septimus up on his offer, it would have been him.

"Why is everyone looking at me?" Pete asked.

"I hope you saved room for dessert," Septimus said.

Pete grinned. "No worries," he said. "There's a special dessert compartment in my stomach that's always empty."

Bob looked at Mallory. Ever since they'd

come down from Septimus's study, she'd seemed a little distant or distracted. He hadn't been able to talk to her, so he didn't know what was going on, but she seemed to be thinking about something other than the dinner they were having.

Still, she *had* told Septimus about her mother's new boyfriend and the fact that, as a child, he'd lived on the commune run by Draven Chandler's parents. After all, Gideon Sawyer had been the source of all the information that Jupiter had given Septimus. He'd been fascinated by all the details – the bloodletting ceremony on the mini-pyramid, the use of that blood in baking sacred bread, the ritual of lowering children into dry wells so that they could supposedly hear the voices of the gods.

"As you probably know," he'd said, "some of that seems to have its roots in customs the Maya actually practiced. They certainly had rituals drenched in blood. But I'm not aware of them putting children in wells to communicate with the gods. That might have been the weird invention of Draven Chandler's father. Though I'm really not an expert on any aspect of Mayan history except the history of explicit zero."

"I imagine that the smallest sound echoes and reverberates in an enclosed space like a well," Jupiter said.

"And how a child's imagination could be so easily primed by the adults," Bob said.

"Yes," Septimus said. "Tell an impressionable child that he or she is going to hear the voices of the gods and then lower him into a dark well with lots of echoes, and who knows what will happen?"

He turned to Mallory. "Did Gideon Sawyer tell your mother any of the things that Draven Chandler said the gods had told him?"

"No," Mallory said. "Not specifically. Just that Chandler was full of himself, as if he'd been specially chosen and was therefore sort of a little god himself."

"I don't know if this Gideon Sawyer will remember," Septimus said. "But if you get the chance to ask him, see if he can recall any distinct messages."

"He probably said something like, 'The gods want me to have special powers'," Pete said. "He could have made up anything he wanted."

"That would be quite convenient, wouldn't it?" Jupiter said seriously. "Who's going to contradict him if the gods told him that?"

"Maybe the gods told him to push his father off the cliff," Pete suggested.

"Frankly," Septimus went on, "when I met Chandler, he didn't strike me as a murderer, but I may be wrong. He seemed to have a split personality — not in the classic sense, but nevertheless. Part of him seemed very cold-blooded, fantastically ambitious, and in love with power. But another part of him seemed a bit childlike. I mean, what you told me about him and Dr. Haldorrson is bonkers. Who gets all their joints replaced ahead of time on the basis of a wacky theory?"

"As far as him being a murderer," Jupiter said, "there's more we haven't told you."

The dining room was shrouded in shadow. The amber-colored drapes that hung at the sides of the windows now framed large rectangles of night. The candlelight and dim glow from the chandelier were not enough to vanquish the pools of darkness that huddled in the corners. Septimus's house was very fancy, but it wasn't very reassuring. With its high ceilings and weirdly angled spaces it raised more questions than it answered. All the talk of murder and wells and sacred bread made of blood was suddenly making Bob feel a little creeped out.

"What do you mean?" Septimus asked Jupiter.

"Well, not murder exactly," Jupiter said. "Let me just call it a suspicious death."

"He means Senator Hayden," Pete said.

"We discovered by doing some research," Jupiter said, "that about fifteen years ago Senator Hayden broke some bones in his foot while playing touch football. It turns out that his most recent trip to the hospital — just a week before he died — was for the very same thing. He supposedly broke the very same bones he'd broken before — though this time while throwing the ball for his dogs."

"The very same bones?" Septimus said. "Well, that's possible. Once the bones are broken, I suspect they don't grow back quite as strongly as they originally were. But I don't know for sure. I'm not an M.D."

"Yes, it's possible," Jupiter said. "But what if the senator wanted to go to the hospital for another reason — one he wanted to keep secret? Then the broken-bones-in-the-foot story would be a great cover. We found out that the doctor that Hayden went to see after he left the foot doctor is a woman named Avery Eden, who is supervising a clinical trial that has to do with cognitive function. We think Hayden may have died as a result of a reaction to an experimental drug.

"We also found out that there's almost certainly an alliance between Byron Baxter, the senator's top aide, and Draven Chandler," Jupiter added. "And when you ask the question of who benefits most from the senator's death, the answer most probably is the two of them. But we're not sure how to catch them."

"Boy," Septimus said. "You guys don't fool around, do you?"

"Well, *sometimes* we do," Pete said. "And before we go any further in our investigations, why don't we investigate that dessert?"

Bob thought Pete was being funny rather than rude, and Septimus seemed to think so too. He was gone from the table for a few minutes, but he soon returned with a three-layer chocolate cake with chocolate icing, and the plates and forks to go along with it.

"Wow!" Pete said. "Does that look great or what?"

"Do you guys want milk to go with this?" Septimus asked.

"Yes, please," Bob said.

Septimus returned with a gallon jug of milk and started filling their empty water glasses. The cake was delicious, but though

Septimus kept urging second pieces on everyone, the simple fact was that they were absolutely stuffed.

"So what are you going to do with all your new information?" Septimus asked. "I expect you're still trying to find a way to help Dr. Haldorrson?"

"Exactly," Jupiter said. "Unfortunately, we're aware that all our conclusions are suppositions and that we don't have any hard proof. We brainstormed about what that hard proof might be, and we suspect that there just isn't any. So we have to make some."

"Why don't we go to the sitting room?" Septimus said. "I think we'll be more comfortable in there."

Bob and Pete started to clear the table, but Septimus was having none of that.

"Just leave everything where it is. I'm having too much fun talking with you to interrupt it."

There was a door leading right from the dining room to the sitting room, and after they blew out the candles on the table, they made their way to the couches and chairs arranged around the perimeter of the room. With the lights on, the room was a lot cozier than the dining room had been, and the spooky feelings that Bob had had evaporated.

When they were all settled in, Jupiter said, "As far as catching Draven Chandler goes, we were actually hoping that you might help us."

Septimus's eyebrows rose. "Really?" he said. "How?"

"We thought it might work if we set up a sting," Jupiter said. "If we got Chandler talking about himself when he was feeling relaxed and self-confident. He might let something slip."

"And you don't think that would happen if you were talking to him?" Septimus said.

Jupiter smiled and shook his head.

"He dropped by the Salvage Yard this morning," Bob told Septimus. "He more or less tricked Jupe into giving him one of our business cards last night, and this morning, there he was, knocking on the door. He said he'd come to reassure us that an investigation was taking place about the accident, but we think he was really just checking us out. We think he considers us a threat and was more or less telling us he had our number."

"So what do you have in mind?" Septimus asked.

"You told us that Chandler got along with you right from the start," Jupiter said, "that you thought he saw in you a kindred spirit. You told us he thinks of himself as one of the masters of the universe, and apparently you're a member of that club, too. So, if the two of you relaxed and started talking, he might just trip up. If we could get the conversation on audio or video, we'd have him. Of course, that would only be true if he said something incriminating. But you'd have to lead him in that direction."

Septimus nodded thoughtfully. "I see what you mean," he said. "Of course it's highly unlikely that he'd just come out and confess that he had anything to do with Senator Hayden's death, but he might say *something*. And I'm beginning to see a way in which I might be able to push things along."

Bob sat forward earnestly, his hands clasped in front of him. The windows in the sitting room were open, and a breeze blew in, stirring the sheer drapes. It had been a bit close in the dining room, and the air was welcome.

"What do you mean?" Jupiter asked.

"I could use my name, for example," Septimus said. "I was talking before about the sides of Chandler's personality. One side is Master of the Universe. But the other is a bit unbalanced, I'd say − a bit superstitious and easily swayed. For example, he told me that one of the reasons he bought the Orion Rigby estate was because both the Italian mansion and the French provincial chateau were haunted. He honestly believes in ghosts – in ethereal presences among us, in ectoplasm. And if those stories about his childhood are true, he may also really believe that the voices of the gods spoke to him when he was put down that well. It would, after all, be nice to feel so special."

"But how would you use your name?" Pete asked. "It's not particularly spooky."

Septimus shifted in the chair he was sitting in. It seemed to Bob that he'd gotten quite interested in the idea of tricking Draven Chandler.

"The four of you may not know this," Septimus said, "but the name was often given to the seventh-born son, who by virtue of his birth order, was supposed to possess a number of talents and was destined for worldly success. And if that seventh son were also to have seven sons, the second Septimus was supposedly gifted with the art of healing and other supernatural powers."

"Are you a seventh son?" Pete asked.

"No," Septimus said. "I'm a first and

only son. My father just really liked the sound of the name. But I'm sure that Draven Chandler would believe my lie."

"There are a lot of interesting things about the number seven, aren't there?" Mallory asked.

"There are indeed," Septimus said. "First of all, it's a prime number, divisible only by itself and the number one. Biologists have discovered that our skin cells slough off and are replaced by new cells every seven days. In western culture, the number seven is considered lucky, mystical, even sacred. It's sometimes called God's number."

"Because the world was supposedly created in seven days?" Pete said.

"Almost," Septimus said. "Supposedly God created the world in six days, and then he rested on the seventh."

"I can see why," Bob said. "That was a lot of heavy lifting."

"There's more," Septimus said.

"Don't tell us, don't tell us," Pete said. "Let's see what we can come up with. Aren't there seven continents?"

"And seven seas," Mallory said.

"Each of the four phases of the moon lasts for seven days," Jupiter said. "And, unless

I have this wrong, there were seven planets in ancient astronomy."

Septimus nodded, sagely. ""Before telescopes got more powerful," he said. "That would be Mercury, Venus, Earth, Mars, Jupiter, Saturn, and Uranus."

"Aren't there seven colors in the rainbow?" Mallory asked.

"And seven notes in the musical scale," Septimus said. "And we mustn't forget the seven deadly sins. Perhaps I can use them when I talk to Draven Chandler."

"Boy," Pete said. "This is weird. No wonder so many people think the number seven is magic."

"I don't know about magic," Septimus said. "But it does have an aura about it. And it would be easy for someone like Draven Chandler to believe that the number seven denoted wisdom, truth, and harmony. Anyway, I could contact Chandler and invite him to come here, oh, say, the day after tomorrow? His conference will be over by then and he won't be so busy or distracted. And he'll probably be feeling very proud of its success, very full of himself. I could say that I wanted to talk with him about some future collaboration concerning the nature of consciousness."

"I bet he'd come," Pete said.

"I bet he would, too," said Jupiter. "And ever since I first heard about your hologram – and even more, now that I've seen it – I've been thinking that you could pretend your hologram is a ghost."

Septimus stared at Jupiter with what Bob could only call deep respect.

"That's a truly terrific idea," he said. "Your father would be proud. Chandler seemed serious to me when he told me he believed in ghosts. I could take him to my study upstairs and show him one."

"Yes," Jupiter said. "I think if you started the process off by filling his head with a lot of stuff about being the seventh son of a seventh son , and then told him that ever since you met him at the Institute, you'd been getting glimpses of a ghostly figure in your study – very lifelike – who's been trying to tell you something about a place called The Place of the Food of the Gods, you might find him remarkably receptive."

"Or remarkably gullible," said Mallory. "Maybe you could say that the ghost sometimes calls the place The Place of the Light Near the Sea."

"That's a good idea," said Jupiter. "You

could say that you've never heard of either of those places, and that you were wondering if Draven Chandler had. I'm sure he'd be pretty protected from saying very much about the senator, but undoubtedly there are chinks in his armor."

"I really like this idea," said Septimus. "A *lot*! I can tell him this ghostly figure seems to know him and says he played some strange game with a ball when they were kids together. Then I can take him up to my study and show him a hologram of someone who looks a bit like this Gideon Sawyer.

"Maybe Gideon Sawyer himself will be willing to pose for the hologram, and I can set up the program to suggest that the ghost *is* Gideon Sawyer, and that he's now dead. If Gideon's willing to help out, then the hologram can talk for a while and then suddenly blurt out that Chandler murdered his father by pushing him off a cliff. That ought to take him by surprise. I can get Draven Chandler's reactions on audio tape, at least."

Jupiter said, "That's a truly terrific plan. It may not work, of course. Draven Chandler might be sufficiently protected that he just sneers at you, but you could still probably use the whole set-up to get him to say something incriminating. It's all a matter of throwing someone off balance and catching them at an undefended moment."

"I bet it *does* work," Bob said, glancing at Mallory. While Septimus and Jupiter had been talking, she'd looked a little bit sick to her stomach. Bob had been waiting all through dinner to ask her what was going on and now he finally asked her straight out.

"Mallory," he said, "ever since we came down from Septimus's study, you've had something on your mind. What's going on?"

"It's just an idea," she said, looking a bit embarrassed. "A sort of theory."

"So tell us," Jupiter said.

She took a deep breath and turned to Septimus. "Remember when you said that seeing the truth was often hard," she asked, "and that when you finally did, it was like pulling back a curtain and finding a door behind it?"

"Yes," Septimus said. "Go on."

"Well, that's what happened to me last night," Mallory said. "Literally. I was interested in discovering how Chandler or whoever had managed to hide all the high tech controls for the lights and the sound and the video. So I pulled back that red velvet curtain at the front of the room. There's an almost invisible door behind it that leads to a room further back in the mansion."

"Yes," Septimus said. "A sort of green room, or holding chamber. That's where Draven Chandler and I were before the lecture. We came to the stage from behind that curtain."

"I saw the way the cable that held up those heavy mirrored balls was connected to a bracket back there," Mallory explained. "Let's suppose that what happened in the ballroom wasn't an accident. Let's say it was attempted murder. What if someone was behind that curtain and noticed my cousin Skinny working right under one of those mirrored balls and saw his chance? All he had to do was rip the cable loose from that bracket. It would look like an accident. As Chandler told us this morning, a catastrophic failure."

"Wow!" Pete said. "You think someone wanted to kill Skinny? Why?"

"I don't know," Mallory said, "but I've thought a lot about who. And it seems almost certain that someone must have been Draven Chandler. If so, he's unbelievably dangerous. If he'd succeeded, it might have been the third death he was responsible for. Jupiter told us that it gets easier and easier to kill the more you do it. So I'm worried about your plan, Septimus. I don't think it would be safe for you to be alone in this big house with a possible murderer, especially one you'd be working hard to get to confess. He may be credulous when it comes to ghosts, and he may be wacky in other regards, but this is a guy who has big dreams of power, and he's certainly capable of acting in his own defense."

"Mallory's right," Pete said. "You'll need backup."

"I'm very impressed by your analysis of the so-called accident with the balls, Mallory," Septimus said, "and what you say gives me pause. I may have been treating this whole affair a bit too cavalierly – not taking Draven Chandler seriously enough. You're quite right that if this is a man who was willing to kill a sitting U.S. senator in order to have a chance at filling his seat, he'd stop at nothing. Holograms are marvelous things, but they don't provide protection from murderers."

"We'll be here too, then," Jupiter said. "We can hide somewhere in the house, in case there's any trouble."

"That's great," Septimus said. "I'll be happy to have you nearby." Bob was really impressed by the way he was treating them – as dinner guests, and now as co-conspirators – as if all of them were adults, just like he was. "But why in the world would Draven Chandler want to kill one of his own interns?"

Bob had been wondering the same thing.

"I've been thinking about it all through dinner," Mallory said. "And the only reason I can come up with is that Skinny knows something that's really incriminating – something he ran across in a phone call or an e-mail in the course of whatever it is he does at the Institute. But here's the thing. Given it's Skinny, whatever he knows means nothing to him. If he thought it was significant in some way, he'd never be able to keep it to himself. He'd be flaunting it and pretending it made him important."

"So you think Skinny knows something he doesn't know he knows," Jupiter said, pinching his bottom lip. "And somehow Draven Chandler knows he knows."

"But when Skinny introduced us to Draven Chandler," Bob said, "it was pretty clear that Chandler didn't recognize Skinny at all. He probably wouldn't have known he worked at the Institute if he hadn't had a STAFF badge. So how could Chandler have gone from knowing nothing about Skinny to wanting to kill him in a couple of hours?"

"That's a good question," Pete said, "but after all, it doesn't take much to make you want to kill Skinny."

"It doesn't really matter what he knows or doesn't know," Jupiter said. "All you need to know is that he's Skinny."

"Yeah, Mallory," Pete said. "You might have finished him off up in Napa when he fell in the hole."

Everyone laughed, but underneath it, Bob could sense that they were trying to make light of a situation that made them all uncomfortable. He remembered Skinny's face the night before, and how terrified he'd been, and how sorry he'd felt for him. "So what do we do?" he asked.

"I think that one or two of us ought to try to talk to Skinny tomorrow," Jupiter said. "Since Mallory and I are the two best actors among the four of us, maybe Bob and Pete can meet with Dr. Haldorrson at the hospital to bring him up to date, while Mallory and I go to the Institute for Eternal Consciousness to talk to Skinny. It might be hard, trying to get him to tell us what he knows. But it's worth a shot."

"That's an excellent idea," Septimus said. "And tomorrow I'll be busy as well. I'll contact Gideon Sawyer, and then, with any luck, spend the day constructing a suitable hologram to put the fear of the gods in Draven Chandler!"

12

What Skinny Doesn't Know He Knows

The next morning, when Worthington arrived at the Salvage Yard to take the four of them on their dual missions, Jupiter was still thinking about how Septimus Halfpenny had appeared, apparently out of nowhere, like an answer to a secret wish. Not only had Septimus been good friends with Jupiter's father, but he was very deeply interested in things that deeply interested Jupiter. The house he was living in suggested a mind that could engage with multiple facets of reality – as did his shift from physics to philosophy. And on top of all that, when Jupiter had suggested that maybe Septimus could spook Draven Chandler into saying more than he meant to by convincing him that Octagon House was haunted by a ghost, he had taken the ball and run with it. The previous evening would stay in Jupiter's mind for a long time to come.

Indeed, Jupiter already had two entirely different but equally happy memories of time spent with Septimus Halfpenny, and if all went well, then in another night or two, The Three

230

Investigators would be working with him on a case. In the meanwhile, they had work of a different kind to do, so as Worthington pulled up at the main entrance to Oceanview Hospital, Jupiter gave Pete and Bob some final instructions.

"We're right on time," he said as Pete and Bob tensed, ready to get out. The hospital looked cold, corporate, and monolithic, a large glass-and-steel rectangle reflecting the late morning sunlight – the kind of place where secret clinical trials were carried out. Jupiter glanced at his watch. "Dr. Haldorrson is expecting you at eleven," he added. "Are you both clear on what your mission is?"

"Sure," Pete said. "We're going to tell Dr. Haldorrson what we've discovered. And what we think."

"Good," Jupiter said. "But don't tell him about our plans to bring in Septimus and Octagon House. And don't forget to ask him if he can get inside information on the drug trials that this Dr. Avery Eden is running."

"We got it, Jupe," Bob said. "Good luck with Skinny."

Jupiter watched as Pete and Bob walked up to the entrance. The automatic sliding glass doors opened and the two of them disappeared from view. Worthington eased away from the curb and soon left the hospital behind.

Jupiter was all alone in the back seat and the extra space gave him an opportunity to stretch and relax. Mallory sat in her customary seat up front with Worthington.

"Did you ask your mother to call her brother?" Jupiter asked Mallory.

"I was there when she called," Mallory said. "Uncle Sylvester said he'd make sure that Skinny would be available during lunchtime to talk to us."

Jupiter glanced at his watch again. They'd be at the Institute with time to spare for their twelve o'clock meeting with Skinny. It would be a challenging interview, Jupiter thought. How to find out what Skinny knew, if he didn't know he knew it?

"You four were a bit quiet on the way back from Septimus Halfpenny's house last night," Worthington said. "What happened?"

"It's a remarkable place," Mallory said. "But you can tell that from the outside."

"I've never seen anything like it," Worthington said. "Did it appeal to you?"

"It appealed to my mind a *lot*," Mallory said. "It's full of surprising and unusual spaces. But I don't think I'd want to live in it."

"I can see why Septimus likes it, though," Jupiter said. "I think it keeps him wide awake. His study takes up the whole top floor — where he also keeps a hologram. Do you know anything about them?" he asked Worthington.

"Only from the movies," Worthington said.

"They're one of Septimus's hobbies," Jupiter said. "He creates them. He has a hologram of Socrates that he showed us, and he and the hologram argue philosophically."

"A question-asking hologram," Worthington said.

"That's right," said Jupiter. "But even before I saw how sophisticated a hologram can be, I was thinking that maybe Draven Chandler could be persuaded it was actually a ghost."

"The thing is," Mallory interjected, "my mother's new boyfriend — a guy named Gideon Sawyer — actually knew Draven Chandler when they were kids. They lived on a very weird commune together. And this morning Septimus was going to call Gideon to ask him if he'd be willing to be the ghost! Jupiter and Septimus both think that if the hologram comes right out and accuses Chandler of killing his father, it ought to shock him sufficiently so that he might say wild things and incriminate himself further."

"It certainly is an audacious idea," Worthington said. "But do you really think it will work?"

"I'm not sure," Jupiter said. "Do you remember a talk we had some time back about the psychology of the individual?"

Worthington nodded. "You noted that the study of character was the linchpin of all good detective work."

Jupiter smiled. Good old Worthington. He'd been there from the very beginning of The Three Investigators – back when he'd driven Jupiter, Pete, and Bob to the offices of the famous British director Reginald Clarke, and afterwards to Terror Castle itself. He'd been there with Bob to rescue him and Pete when they'd been tied up by Stephen Terrill and his friend in disguise. Right from the start he'd been someone Jupiter could talk to. His affection for the man was long and deep. It was great to think that his developing interest in Septimus Halfpenny in no way meant that his relationship with Worthington would be affected.

"Yes," Jupiter said. "And it seems to me that Draven Chandler has a pretty complex psychology and character. One of life's mysteries is the interaction of human character and intelligence, and Draven Chandler is very, very smart."

"Not only that," Mallory said, "but Septimus was commenting on how there seem to be two very different sides to him. He can be coldly scientific and analytical and intellectual, and drawn to power and influence, but he's also got a squishier side — he's apparently very superstitious, given to kooky theories and a belief in ghosts."

"He sounds like one of your trickier villains," Worthington said.

"And that's the proper word in this case," Jupiter said. "A lot of the other bad guys we've caught have simply been greedy or selfish or simply misguided. But Draven Chandler seems to be someone who doesn't stop at murder. He's got a long-term plan, and he's patient, and ruthless. He may be a hard nut to crack."

"Unlike Skinny," Mallory said.

Worthington laughed. "Remember when he was parked outside your apartment at the Wessex House and I'd brought you back there with your new immigrant's trunk? I got him to leave with little trouble."

"And fast!" Mallory said, grinning. "He

really stepped on the gas."

"I'm sure the two of you will be quite successful," Worthington said.

"I'm *not* so sure," Jupiter said. "We don't have a plan, really. We're just going to wing it. But Skinny's guard will be up. It's too bad there's been so much friction and taunting and jabbing between him and us over the years. Trying to get him to cooperate won't be easy. He may envy us but he doesn't like us. Whereas Draven Chandler does like and trust Septimus."

Worthington looked directly in the rear view mirror and caught Jupiter's eye.

"I'd be more than willing to help," he said. "With Skinny, I mean. It worked once before, and, as you'll remember, I managed to use my acting skills on a case of yours last summer."

That was true, Jupiter remembered. Worthington had done a terrific job when he'd posed as a gambler to get information from Jimmy Littlewolf's half-brother at the casino.

"That would be great, Worthington," he said. Mallory nodded enthusiastically. "But what would you do?"

"Hmmm," Worthington said. "Let me think." They drove for a few minutes in silence as Worthington thrummed his fingers on the steering wheel.

"How about this?" he finally said. "It's a bit of a stretch, but remember, it's Skinny Norris we're talking about. Why don't I take the lead by telling Skinny that when I heard what had happened to him the other night, I'd been very concerned."

"So far, so good," Mallory said. "He'd believe *you* were concerned before he believed *we* were."

Still thrumming his fingers on the steering wheel, Worthington went on. "I'll tell him that a young friend of mine who lived in London had had an accident very much like Skinny's. He'd been at a disco and one of those balls had fallen and almost hit him, and he'd died soon after."

"From injuries?" Mallory asked.

"Invisible injuries," Worthington said, smiling broadly. "Apparently some of these disco balls have a toxic slow-acting gas inside them. No one expects they'll break – much less in the vicinity of someone's head! But the gas poisoned my young friend and killed him. That's why I'm concerned. The poison gas is sometimes so slow-acting that it takes a long time to have its effect. I'll ask Skinny if he feels all right."

"Brilliant," Mallory said, laughing. "He'll be so freaked out he won't even stop to ask if your story makes sense."

"And why shouldn't it?" Jupiter said. "Those disco balls have to have something inside them. Why *not* poison gas?"

At this, Worthington laughed, too. "Then I can say that the two of you are very concerned about him as well, and that's why you wanted to see him," he said. "I can say that the first sign of poisoning is damage to the short-term memory. It's possible that the ball that fell near him didn't have poison gas, but the best way to find out if he's in serious danger is to test his memory."

Jupiter thought that what Worthington had come up with was both beautiful and simple, like all truly great ideas. While it was always dangerous to predict the future, given the psychology of the individual in this particular case, Jupiter was willing to bet quite a bit that Skinny would readily believe this patently ridiculous story of Worthington's. Soon, Worthington was driving through the Institute's gates and heading toward the main building. Perhaps because it was the final day of the conference, the guards were more relaxed. Jupiter and Mallory showed off their GUEST tags and were quickly let through.

Worthington parked and Jupiter led the three of them up the steps of the mansion and into the elaborate foyer. A long table, covered with a white tablecloth, had been placed in front of one of the stairways to the mezzanine, and two young women with STAFF name tags sat behind it.

"Can we help you?" one of them asked pleasantly as Jupiter and Mallory approached.

"Yes," Mallory said. "We're here to see my cousin. He's an intern with the Institute this summer. He was almost hurt the other night in that accident in the ballroom, and we wanted to check on him."

The two women conferred with one another. "Do you mean Eddie?" she asked.

"Eddie?" Mallory said, startled. "I call him Skinny."

"Tall and thin, with a big Adam's apple? He's probably on lunch break now," the other one said. "In the Staff Room." She directed them to a corridor off the right end of the foyer and told them the room was about halfway down and well-marked.

Jupiter, Mallory, and Worthington found it easily. They had no sooner opened the door and walked in when they saw Skinny sitting at a table, alone, eating a sandwich. The minute he saw them, he looked offended. "What are you doing here?" he snarled. "My father said you were coming, but why?"

"Skinny," Mallory said, instantly hostile. "Or should I say Eddie? We just want to ask you a few questions."

Jupiter thought that Worthington's idea had been a lifesaver. He and Mallory would have had an impossible time controlling themselves, even if they *were* trying to act.

"Actually," Worthington said in his very best posh accent, "we are worried about you." He looked like a model English butler, concerned, eager to be of assistance, totally at his master's service. "I don't imagine anyone has told you, but you're still in danger."

"Really?" Skinny said scornfully. "Is a lightning bolt going to strike me down dead?"

"Nothing as silly as that," Worthington said. "I was worried about the poison gas."

Skinny's face twitched.

"You see, sometimes those disco balls like the ones that fell the other night have a gas inside them to make them lighter. It's toxic to humans. A friend of mine was killed by it in London." Grief briefly crossed Worthington's face.

Skinny was beginning to look uneasy. He was blinking rapidly and frowning. "You mean the gas got out when the balls smashed?"

Worthington nodded. "And you would have been in the most danger because you were right there. Do you remember smelling anything unusual?" He sat forward intently.

"No," Skinny said. "Poison gas?"

Worthington kept nodding. "It's usually odorless," he said. "You may have inhaled it without even knowing."

Skinny put his hand to his throat and he turned an even ghastlier shade of white. "You think I might be a goner?" he asked.

"No, no," Worthington said soothingly. "At least not yet. The first thing that happens is that you begin to lose your short-term memory. So we ought to test you a little. If you're having trouble remembering, we should rush you to the hospital."

"I'm too young to die," Skinny said. Jupiter could see he was already beginning to feel hugely sorry for himself.

"Do you remember the name of the man who runs this place?" Worthington said.

"You mean Draven Chandler?" Skinny said, his voice high.

"Good, good," Worthington said.

Skinny looked reverently at the great and beneficent Mr. William Worthington. Jupiter tried to keep himself from smiling. There was no reason for him to say anything. Worthington had the situation firmly under control. He went on to ask about other people Skinny worked with, about how long he'd been working, about what he enjoyed most and least about his job. Skinny eagerly answered each question and kept looking for Worthington's reassurance that maybe he wasn't dying after all.

"So far so good," Worthington said. "You're doing very well. There's reason for hope. Now cast your mind back to the night before last, the night of the accident. It may help if you close your eyes."

Dutifully Skinny's eyes snapped shut. Jupiter thought Mallory was going to break out laughing.

What had Skinny been doing when the balls fell? Worthington asked. Where had he been standing? Did he remember anyone going behind the curtain or coming out from behind it? Any sounds coming from there? Did he hear a door close, perhaps?

He'd just been helping to clean up the ballroom, Skinny said. He'd been near the

front, right in the middle. He'd heard a series
of thwack, thwack, thwacks, and he'd sensed
something above him, and he'd looked up and
just had had time to jump out of the way, and
the thing had smashed all to smithereens, and
the poison gas − . He took a deep breath. No,
he hadn't seen anyone going in or out, but he
did remember hearing a door close in the sudden silence after the balls had shattered.

"Very good," Worthington said. "I think
you may have suffered only minimal damage.
Just a few more questions, all right?"

"Sure," Skinny said eagerly. He looked
at Worthington as if he could, with a sweep of
his arm, remove Skinny's death sentence.

"These last questions involve any odd or
strange or peculiar memories you might have
of the last several weeks. If you have no trouble
with them, we can put away any fears about
your well-being."

"Such as?" Skinny asked.

"Such as what is the most peculiar
phone call you've received since you began
work at the Institute?"

Skinny looked as delighted as if he'd cor-
rectly answered the last question on *Who Wants
To Be A Millionaire*? "That's easy," he said.
"Some guy called up last week and asked if we

killed people and then put them in a deep freeze. He was in good shape now, he said, so he thought that if he died and was preserved for like five hundred years, when he woke up everyone would know how to live forever. He wanted to know if we did that sort of thing and if we could guarantee he'd stay frozen."

"What did you tell him?" Worthington said.

"I told him no," Skinny retorted. "We're not crazy here."

That was the right answer, Jupiter thought. Of course they didn't. Draven Chandler and his transhumanist friends believed in staying alive now — long enough until the secret of immortality was discovered — not in coming to life again in 500 years.

"I hope you were polite to him," Jupiter said. He couldn't help himself.

"What's it to you?" Skinny scowled before turning back deferentially to Worthington.

And the strangest e-mail?

The strangest e-mail Skinny had read had come from a supposedly certified and authorized ghost-finder who, for a fee, guaranteed that he could locate and photograph the ghosts that had accompanied their habitations from Italy and Provence. In *that* case, he'd asked his direct supervisor what he ought to do with the e-mail, and at her suggestion, he'd forwarded it on to Draven Chandler himself. The supervisor thought there was a very good chance that Chandler would hire the guy.

Hmmm, Jupiter thought. Maybe the plan he and Septimus had come up to scare him with a drummed up hologram-ghost might be exactly the right way to get to Draven Chandler, after all.

"One last question," Worthington said. "What's the oddest thing you've seen since you started working here?" He sat back and crossed his arms on his chest as though he were conducting a job interview.

"The oddest thing?" Skinny said. "Jeez, I don't know. There's a lot of them extually. I mean, it's a pretty weird place, if you want to know the truth. You really wouldn't believe how strange some of the people who come here are – not to mention the people who work here. Some of the ones who drop by are even famous, but all of them are peculiar."

"What about the famous ones?" Worthington asked encouragingly.

Yes, Jupiter thought. That was the right question.

"Well," Skinny said, scratching his head

as his Adam's apple bobbed. "One day last week when I was just finishing up for the day, I saw that Senator Hayden guy – you know the one who's dead now? – anyway, he drove up with a man and a woman who were here the other night."

"The night of the accident?" Worthington asked.

"Yeah," Skinny said. He gestured at Jupiter and Mallory. "In fact, the two of them and their other geek friends were talking to them."

Byron Baxter and Mia Osaka, Jupiter thought.

"Anyway," Skinny went on, "the senator dude was wearing this big black boot on his right foot, and the three of them went to sit on the patio outside the ballroom. I saw them because I was helping to set up for the conference. I was looking out the windows at them when Hayden leaned over and took off that boot thing and then wiggled his foot at the two of them. That was weird enough. But then he took off his shoe – the one that was on the other foot – and then he went out onto the grass and started jumping around like he had ants in his pants. The guy and the girl with him rushed over and grabbed his arms and practically dragged him back to the patio."

"An odd memory, indeed," Worthington said.

"Wait!" Skinny said. "There's more. The two of them were arguing with him and waving their hands around and picking up the boot and giving it to him, and he kept shaking his head and pushing it back at them. Finally, he just gave in and put it back on. Though it beats me why he needed it in the first place if he could jump around like he did."

"Very peculiar," Worthington said. "Did you happen to mention this to anyone?"

"I don't think so," Skinny said. "I was all by myself in the ballroom, and it was time to go home." He frowned. "No, wait a minute. Yes. I did tell someone. Not at the time, but the other night, at the opening of the conference. When I saw the guy and the girl again, I remembered what had happened, and I think I may have mentioned it to Draven Chandler."

"May have or did have?" Worthington asked.

"Jeez," Skinny said, looking a little ashamed. "No, I did." He looked at Jupiter and Mallory with a mixture of envy and scorn. He opened his mouth to speak and then shut it again. He opened it and shut it, like a fish out of water.

"What is it, Skinny?" Worthington asked.

"When the boss came up, I had to introduce the four of them and I told him they called themselves investigators. He took their business card." He sneered. "So when I saw him later, I told him that they weren't the only game in town. I told him I was an investigator, too, and that I could do some super investigations every now and then. I told him I'd seen some strange goings-on at the Institute and I could keep my eyes open for him. When he asked me what I'd seen, I told him about the senator."

"Ahh," Worthington said, a long sigh that sounded like the air escaping from a bicycle tire. "It's excellent that you were able to remember that, and so many other things as well. Now, I'm no doctor, but I really think your short-term memory's in fine shape and you can stop worrying about being poisoned. Either you didn't inhale it or there wasn't any poison gas to begin with, but either way, I think you'll live to a fine old age. And if you keep working here, who knows how old that will be?" He laughed.

"Really?" Skinny said. "Boy, that's a

load off."

"Really," Worthington said. His voice was firm and reassuring. "You can just resume your normal life."

"Thanks a million," Skinny said. He shook Worthington's hand fervently. And then he seemed to realize that Worthington had come with Jupiter and Mallory, and if it hadn't been for them, he'd never have gotten a clean bill of health. "And thanks for bringing him," he muttered under his breath.

"What was that, Skinny?" Jupiter said. "I didn't hear you."

"I said thanks for bringing him," Skinny said. "I got to get back to work, now that I'm not going to die. See you later, punks."

He threw the rest of the sandwich he hadn't eaten in the trash and waltzed out of the room, free and easy.

Mallory laughed and clapped Worthington on the back. "You were great!" she said. "Academy Award material."

"Really, Worthington," Jupiter said. "You were incredible."

Worthington looked very pleased. "It was nothing," he said. "A good bit of fun."

The three of them laughed all the way back to the Flex, but even as he laughed, Jupiter couldn't help also feeling sorry for Skinny. It must be terrible to be him, he thought – so riven by jealousy and resentment and anger, so insecure and eager for reassurance, so unhappy in his own skin. It must be terrible to live your life with a mind so clouded by illogic and emotion.

At least they'd gotten what they'd come for, Jupiter thought. It simply couldn't be a coincidence that just a few hours after Skinny had told Draven Chandler what he'd seen Senator Hayden do that the balls had been ripped from the ceiling and had almost killed him. Though Skinny had had no idea what the story about Senator Hayden and the boot meant, Draven Chandler surely did.

Mallory had been right. Skinny knew something that might be dangerous to Draven Chandler, and he'd pulled the bracket securing the cable to the wall and then had left through the concealed door. Poor Skinny! He'd actually bragged to his soon-to-be-attempted murderer that *he* could investigate things, too! And while he wasn't in danger from poison gas, Draven Chandler still knew what he knew.

It didn't make Jupiter happy to reflect that he'd been right when he'd suggested that it might get easier for a killer to kill the more frequently he did it. If Septimus Halfpenny could get things properly set up for his proposed interview with Chandler, they would all have to be quick on their feet, and very careful that nothing went awry.

Meanwhile, they had to go back to Oceanview to pick up Pete and Bob. He couldn't wait to tell the two of them how great Worthington had been, and what they'd learned. Still, on the drive, he found his mind wandering back to the evening before, when Septimus had been showing his guests his Socrates hologram in action. When Septimus had said, "You might as well ask me 'What is the nature of truth'?'", the hologram, sitting on his throne, looking skeptical, had responded "What *is* the nature of truth?" – at which point Septimus had turned the hologram off.

It was funny, Jupiter reflected, that he and Septimus had both been thinking about truth so much, at a time when the plan to get the bad guy involved a lot of lying. Lying by Worthington, Jupiter, and Mallory when they confused Skinny Norris even more than he was confused already, and also lying by Septimus – when the time came – to the extremely devious and clever Draven Chandler.

Of course, the sort of truth Socrates and

other philosophers pursued was of a different nature from the kind people ignored, contravened, and infringed upon every day – and if it weren't for the occasional careful lie, a lot of important everyday-sorts-of-truths would never come to light. But although everyday-sorts-of-truths were very important, Jupiter thought that when Socrates asked about the nature of truth, what he was asking about was the sort of truth that could never be covered up in the end. The sort that was eternal, unchanging, and absolute.

13

Come Into My Parlor, Said The Spider To The Fly

At that moment, at Oceanview Hospital, Pete was standing with Bob outside the portico, on the sidewalk lining the circular drive. They'd been waiting some time now, and Pete was getting hot and bored. "Where's Worthington?" he said. "Look what time it is."

"Maybe they had a harder time with Skinny than they thought they'd have," Bob said.

"Yeah," Pete said. "Even when Skinny *knows* he knows something, he doesn't know it. Imagine how hard it is when he doesn't know he knows it."

Pete picked up a small rock and tried to play hacky sack with it, but it hit his ankle and really hurt. As he let the rock fall to the ground, he thought back to their meeting with Freya's father. Dr. Haldorrson had seemed quite interested in what they'd learned about Senator Hayden and Dr. Avery Eden. But, on the whole, he and Bob had accomplished nothing that couldn't have been done just as well on the phone, and Pete wished that they'd gone with the others to the Institute of Eternal Consciousness instead.

"Here they come," Bob said, pointing. Pete shaded his eyes and stared down the hospital drive. Sure enough, the Flex was almost there. He'd know that car anywhere.

Mallory was in the front with Worthington again, and Jupiter was alone in the back. Bob and Pete piled in on either side of him and they started back toward Rocky Beach.

"So how did it go?" Pete asked.

"Very well," Jupiter said. "Thanks to Worthington's astonishing performance."

"What performance?" Pete asked.

"Worthington came up with a very clever plan to make Skinny believe there was poison gas inside the disco balls and that when they broke, Skinny might have inhaled the gas," Jupiter explained. "The only way to find out was to test his memory. So Worthington asked him a series of leading questions he'd never have answered if Mallory or I had asked them. He thought he was saving his life by being cooperative."

"Wow!" said Pete. "What a great idea!" He could see Worthington smiling in the rear view mirror and clapped him on the shoulder.

"We're lucky Worthington stopped acting," Jupiter said. "He was obviously very good at it."

"Thank you, Master Jones," Worthington said, in his best British chauffeur's accent. "But I certainly am glad I stopped in time to meet the four of you."

"So what did you find out?" Bob asked.

"That Skinny got a call from some guy who wanted the Institute to kill him and freeze him," Mallory said.

"You're kidding!" Pete said.

"He also saw Senator Hayden sitting on the patio outside the ballroom with Byron Baxter and his girlfriend," Jupiter told him. "He was wearing that big black boot I told you about, but he took it off and started dancing around. And it seems that Skinny was jealous enough of the fact that Draven Chandler had asked for a Three Investigators card that he bragged about how he was an investigator, too, and had seen some strange goings-on at the Institute. When Chandler asked him what he'd seen, Skinny told him about the senator and thereby almost signed his own death warrant," Jupiter concluded.

"Luckily, not *quite*," added Mallory.

"Yes," Jupiter said. "Anyway, Skinny

managed to corroborate two of our hypotheses – that Hayden's foot was never broken and that he went to Oceanview Hospital for another reason altogether, and also that Chandler had a compelling motive to try to kill Skinny."

"So not only did Skinny not know the meaning of what he'd seen," Pete said admiringly, "but he also got totally smoked by Worthington!"

"Always remember, Pete," Worthington said. "It's a dangerous world, and there's poison gas lurking everywhere."

"I felt sorry for Skinny the other night," Bob said, "and I still do."

"I do as well," Jupiter said. "It must be hell to be Skinny."

Pete was surprised to hear that Bob and Jupiter had sympathy for E. Skinner Norris. Pete usually had sympathy for anyone in trouble, for any underdog or little guy, but he really had a hard time summoning up any for Skinny.

"I'm glad the three of you had so much success," Pete said, "because what Bob and I found out isn't definite in any way at all. We told Dr. Haldorrson about the commune and the suspicions that Chandler had killed his father, and also about Skinny and the accident. We asked him if he'd call Dr. Eden's department and say he had a patient who wanted in on a drug trial for brain power."

Jupiter frowned.

"Don't worry, Jupe," Bob assured him. "We followed your advice and used the term 'cognitive enhancement.'"

"Dr. Haldorrson talked to Dr. Eden herself," Pete said. "He told her his patient was in his late sixties and basically quite healthy, but that he was getting his hip replaced, and also starting to have memory lapses, and that he wanted to try anything that might help."

"Dr. Eden told Dr. Haldorrson that the patient sounded as if he might qualify," Bob added. "She said they were accepting healthy people over fifty who were starting to suffer cognitive impairment. But they couldn't be taking any drugs that might react badly with the test drug. She said they'd been testing the drug in England and that nine patients had died of sudden heart attacks before the doctors running the trial figured out that all the people who died had been taking a certain painkiller. So she said that anyone in the trial she was administering had to sign an affidavit swearing that they weren't taking that drug."

"While I agree with Pete that that isn't absolutely definitive," said Jupiter, "it's certainly suggestive. If you wanted to kill somebody, you'd have a pretty good chance of doing so if you were able to enroll them in a drug trial that required no cross-mixing of certain drugs and then you managed to secretly give them the drug that would kill them. Say you were a trusted top aide to the person. If Byron Baxter managed to make sure the Senator took this painkiller, there's little to no chance that they could ever prove what happened without the help of a good forensic unit or crime scene investigation. "

"But how could Baxter have given him this other drug, do you think?" Pete asked.

"Maybe he crushed it and put it in a drink," Jupiter said, "or made him think it was something else, like a vitamin or herbal remedy. Or maybe Dr. Granger prescribed it and the senator just took it because he'd been told to."

Pete sat back, resting his elbow on the open window and letting his hand wave in the wind the Flex created. The rest of the way back to Rocky Beach, Jupiter was quiet and sat pinching his lip, but Pete was thinking of little but how hungry he suddenly felt.

When they arrived at the Salvage Yard, they thanked Worthington again for all his help and went into HQ2. Pete headed straight for the small kitchen in the back.

"I don't know about the rest of you," he said, "but I'm starving. It's after one o'clock and we haven't had any lunch."

They all followed Pete who laid out eight slices of bread on the counter, slathered four of them with peanut butter and jelly, then topped them with another piece of bread before cutting them in half. "Come and get it," he said, as he poured four glasses of milk.

As he was eating his sandwich, Jupiter wandered over to the office section where a red light was blinking on the phone. "We have a message," Jupiter called to the others. "Come over as soon as you finish eating." He picked up the phone, pressed the button, and listened to the message.

When Pete had washed down the last mouthful with the last gulp of milk, he went over and joined Jupiter. "Who called?" he asked.

"Septimus," Jupiter said. "He wants us to call him back."

As soon as everyone was gathered, Jupiter dialed the number and pressed the speaker-phone button. They could all hear the phone ring. Pete wondered where the phone was in that huge house, and if Septimus could even hear it. But he had heard it; he picked up after the seventh ring – had he planned that? Pete wondered – and told them that everything was all set for the following evening.

"Draven Chandler was very cordial," Septimus said. "He seemed pleased to get the invitation. He's due here tomorrow at about eight o'clock or so, just as it's starting to get dark."

"What did you tell him?" Jupiter asked.

"I said how impressed I'd been by the Institute, and how much I'd enjoyed giving the lecture and talking to people afterwards," Septimus said. "I told him I thought we might work together on some future projects, and I wanted to talk to him about the possibilities. By the time he gets here, everything will be ready in my study."

"Do you mean – ," Jupiter asked.

"The new hologram will be ready," Septimus said. "When Gideon Sawyer understood that the subject of my inquiry was Draven Chandler, he was eager to help. He immediately grasped the idea of the hologram and agreed that it would have a good chance of working, given Chandler's unusual proclivities. He didn't know if Chandler would remember him or recognize him, but he sent me a bunch of photographs of himself, taken when he was slightly younger."

"And you can use those pictures to make your hologram?" Pete asked.

"Indeed," Septimus said. "I'm working on it. By tomorrow night I'll have the hologram all ready to go, as well as an audio device to capture everything that's said in the room."

Pete was beginning to get excited. He agreed with Jupiter that this Draven Chandler would be dangerous if cornered, and they'd have to be careful and on their guard. But the whole thing also sounded like a lot of fun – with them hiding in the Octagon House to act as witnesses and to be ready in case anything went awry.

Pete loved surveillance, and some of his fondest Three Investigators' memories involved him and his friends tailing suspects. Add to that the idea of a manufactured ghost and Pete was all in on this. He wasn't sure how he felt about ghosts in general, and in spite of everything Jupiter had tried to drum into his head over the years, he still wasn't completely sure they didn't exist. But he knew that the ghost on the third floor of Septimus Halfpenny's house wouldn't be a ghost at all but just a bunch of reflected or refracted light.

Jupiter and Septimus were winding up their conversation. "You four should get here by 6:30 or 7:00," Septimus said, "so we'll have plenty of time to go over everything. If Chandler is on time, then he and I can talk for a few minutes, and it ought to be totally dark by the time we go upstairs."

"We'll plan on that," Jupiter said.

"Great," Septimus said. "I'm getting back to work on the ghost. See you tomorrow. Goodbye."

Jupiter hung up the phone. Pete looked from Bob to Mallory to Jupe. All his friends seemed to feel the way he did – keyed up, excited, a bit apprehensive. How was he going to get through the next thirty hours or so without exploding? he wondered.

In the end, it wasn't as bad as Pete had feared. The next day, he worked much of the morning and early afternoon at the Animal Rescue Center – where he was helping to train a new bunch of volunteers. While he did this, Mallory was working at the Salvage Yard, Bob was at the library, and Jupiter was helping his aunt and uncle.

The day passed quickly, and after dinner and a quick rest at home, Pete met the others back at the Salvage Yard to wait for Worthington. He was right on time. Now, they were all quiet with anticipation as they drove up the gravel drive that led to the Octagon House.

Pete glanced at his watch. It was 6:47. Septimus had said between 6:30 and 7:00, so they were on time. Still, it didn't seem to Pete as though an hour was enough to get everything in order.

"Good luck," Worthington said as he put the car back into DRIVE. "Call me if you need me."

Septimus opened the front door even before they'd mounted the curving stairs to the wraparound porch. He ushered them into the entry hall. "Excellent," he said. "You're here. Everything's in place. Come on upstairs."

He led the way to the second floor and then to the third. The big octagonal room was lit only by a standing lamp in back of an easy chair by Septimus's desk and by the waning light of day.

Pete's eye was drawn to a black orb about the size of a grapefruit on Septimus's desk. He started laughing.

"Is that what I think it is?" he asked.

"A Magic 8 ball?" Septimus said. "Very helpful for making quick decisions."

"I *love* those things!" Pete said. "Outcome uncertain."

"Well, that pretty well sums up tonight," Jupiter said.

Pete saw that Septimus had repositioned the big throne-like chair that the hologram of Socrates had appeared to sit in.

"Is that where – " he asked.

"I think the image of Gideon Sawyer is quite convincing," Septimus said. "I'd love to show it to you now, but it's all set up and ready to go, and I'd have to re-jigger the program, so I'd better not."

"That's fine," Jupiter said. "So long as you're convinced."

Septimus nodded vigorously. "Oh, I am, indeed. And I think that Draven Chandler will be convinced as well. By the way, I've decided to let him believe I own this house. No reason to tell him the truth, if he doesn't know it already." He moved to the large built-in closet that took up most of one of the eight sides of the room and opened the door. It was about three feet deep, and Pete could see that it had been emptied of whatever had been in it and the floor padded with blankets.

"I think the four of you should divide into two teams," Septimus said. "I'll want two of you downstairs with me, for when Chandler first arrives. There's no audio set-up down there, and I'll need witnesses in case anything important gets said. And then the other two should sequester yourselves in this closet. I think it'll be dark enough so you can leave the door open a bit. It's a little tight, but in case anything goes wrong with the audio, you'll want to listen carefully, too, so you can testify later."

Pete volunteered to stay downstairs. The closet looked small and uncomfortable, and though it might well be the more exciting assignment, he saw no reason why he and whoever he was with couldn't sneak up the stairs and listen from below. He was glad when Bob said he'd join him. So Mallory and Jupiter would overhear the haunting of Draven Chandler.

They all went back downstairs. The Tea Room was a smallish triangular room in the back right-hand corner of the house, wedged between the dining room and the sitting room, with doors leading to both. Septimus suggested that Pete and Bob hide in there, behind the door, with the door open.

That would keep them out of sight, but they'd be able to hear everything, and even see a little through the gap between the door and doorjamb. If for some unforeseen reason, Draven Chandler decided to go into the Tea Room, they could escape through the other doors into the dining room. It struck Pete as a good plan. At least they wouldn't be cramped the way Jupiter and Mallory would be upstairs.

They fell into chairs in the sitting room where they joked nervously and tried to relax. They were all surprised when they heard a car approaching the house. Its headlights raked the porch and shone briefly through the sitting room windows. It was 7:45 by Pete's watch. Draven Chandler was early.

"Yikes!" Pete said, jumping to his feet. Bob followed him into the Tea Room as Mallory and Jupiter sprinted down the long hall to the entry, and then up the stairs to the third floor. When the knock sounded, four distinct assertive raps, Pete and Bob were hidden behind the Tea Room door. Pete was almost trembling. The knocks were distant but Pete could hear them well in the absolute stillness of the house.

"Draven," said Septimus. "Welcome."

The voices came closer as the two men walked down the hall toward the sitting room.

"This is a remarkable house," Draven Chandler said. "I'm impressed."

"And that from the man who owns the Orion Rigby estate," Septimus said cordially.

"No," Chandler said. "This is truly an extraordinary place." The two men were in the sitting room now, and Septimus was offering Chandler something to drink and Chandler was refusing.

"The Octagon House called to me," Septimus said when the two men were seated. "I felt from the start that there was something mystical about it and its almost circular shape. Thoughts, images, and feelings never hit a wall; they just go around and around at ever-increasing speed. It's like a spiritual super-colliding superconductor."

"Interesting," Chandler said. "So, you're drawn to the mystical?"

"As the seventh son of a seventh son," Septimus said.

Chandler interrupted him. "You're kidding," he said.

"No," Septimus said mildly. "I was born with special powers. I never asked for them, Lord knows, but I've learned to live with them, to balance them against my scientific bent. I think that's what brought me to think about the sentience of the cosmos. I'm actually quite psychic."

Draven Chandler's voice rose in excitement. Pete peered through the tiny gap between the door and jamb, but all he could see was Draven Chandler's shoes. "As you know," he was saying, "I'm very involved in the science of aging and the search for the secrets of immortality. So naturally I'm drawn to questions about what happens to us if we *do* die."

"Yes," Septimus said. "You told me so the other night. You mentioned that both your mansion and your chateau were haunted."

"Or so the story went," Chandler said. "So far I've been disappointed. No manifestations as of yet. I even hired a certified spirit locater, but he's come up empty."

"That's too bad," Septimus said. "But if I were a ghost, I might have preferred to stay in Europe too."

Chandler chuckled appreciatively.

"I'm pretty sure our spirits linger," Septimus went on. "I wasn't surprised to discover that this house actually has a ghost — an added bonus the estate agent didn't mention." He laughed lightly.

"Really?" Chandler said, obviously intrigued.

"I think so," Septimus said. "Recently, when I've been at work in my study, up on the third floor, I've several times heard a semi-audible voice. Nothing too distinct. And once or twice I've seen this ghostly figure sitting in this one particular chair. A bit angry, even accusatory."

"Do you think it might manifest tonight?" Chandler asked.

"I have no idea," Septimus said. "He seems to come and go at his own whim."

"Perhaps we could go up and see?" Chandler said.

Pete was very impressed with the ease with which Septimus had managed to steer the conversation; he'd been so convincing that Pete was even starting to think there really might be a ghost who lived in the house. What Septimus had said about the circularity of the place made sense, and how bits and pieces of spirit would just go around and around, speeding up until they coalesced and became visible. He almost got the shivers thinking about it.

Bob was behind him, breathing on his neck, but Pete found the closeness comforting at the moment. He reminded himself that this was all a story that Septimus had cooked up, and that he was too old to believe in the sorts of silly things he'd believed in earlier in his life. Or almost too old.

"Certainly we can go up," Septimus said. "But I'd hate to disappoint you. I may be wrong. And the previous owner seems never to have been haunted. A very nice man by the name of Gideon Sawyer. I was sorry to hear that he'd died not long after he sold me the house."

"Did you say Gideon Sawyer?" Chandler asked. Pete could tell the name was familiar to him.

"Yes," Septimus said.

"Do you happen to know anything about him?" Chandler asked.

"No," Septimus said, "Sorry. I know nothing at all, other than that he owned this house."

"Do you know how he died?" Chandler asked.

Pete presumed he was referring to the belief that people who died violently and unexpectedly, with unfinished business, were more likely to come back as ghosts.

"I have no idea," Septimus said. "I found out only belatedly because of some unfinished paperwork having to do with the sale."

"Maybe the ghost is this Gideon Sawyer," Chandler mused. "That would make sense, no? *My* ghosts are supposed to be past residents of the mansion and chateau."

Septimus said nothing, and Pete could see that, as the familiar saying went, he was giving Chandler enough rope to hang himself.

"The odd thing is I knew a boy by that name when I was a child," Chandler said. Pete could sense his growing excitement. Septimus had been extremely clever, baiting the trap and drawing him in slowly.

"That would be quite a coincidence," Septimus said. "Though stranger things have happened."

Pete could hear Chandler getting to his feet. "You've piqued my curiosity," he said to Septimus. "I know you wanted to talk about future business ventures or collaborations, but do you think we could go upstairs first? It's dark now and my own experience suggests that just after night has fallen is the best time to get in touch with psychic phenomena."

Septimus stood too, and his voice was jovial and accommodating. "Sure," he said. "I can't promise anything, but on the way I can show you the rest of the house."

And they were gone, out of the sitting room and down the hall toward the flight of stairs to the second floor.

Neither Pete not Bob moved until they

couldn't hear anything any more, and then they stepped away from the door they'd been hiding behind. Pete couldn't believe how tense he was from having stood so motionless for so long. His shoulders hurt, and his legs were partly asleep.

"Septimus was amazing, wasn't he?" he whispered.

"He sure was," Bob said, grinning. "He's got Chandler right where he wants him."

"Let's wait a few more minutes and then go upstairs," Pete suggested. "I don't want to be left out."

"Me neither," Bob said, and then he reached out and jostled Pete's arm. "That's long enough. I'm sure they're up in the study by now."

"O.K.," Pete said. "Let's go." They began to walk slowly and stealthily to the stairs, and then began to creep up them.

14

The Ghost of Gideon Sawyer

When Mallory and the others saw the approach of Draven Chandler's car, she and Jupiter had hurried out of the sitting room and up to the study. They'd been sitting on the floor of the closet ever since, side-by-side, their backs against the wall, the doors just barely open and their legs splayed out in front of them, waiting. They'd decided not to talk – not even to whisper, though Mallory had long known that she and Jupiter could communicate without words if necessary – a raised eyebrow, a gesture, a pointed look. They understood each other.

The room's only light came from the floor lamp by Septimus's desk. Jupiter sat staring straight ahead, deep in thought, his face in shadow. Mallory was thinking too – about Gideon Sawyer. Her mother had only known him for a few days, and yet he'd gone out of his way to help when Septimus called and explained what they had planned.

Of course, she thought, he wasn't a big fan of Draven Chandler's. Still, it was great of him to help them. She wondered if Septimus

273

and Gideon might become friends after working together on this project to trap The Man Who Wished To Live Forever.

She was startled out of her reverie by the sound of voices. They were still some distance away; it seemed that Septimus was giving Chandler a tour of the second floor. Jupiter had heard the voices too and he acted quickly to secure the closet doors. As he and Mallory settled in, she silently thanked Septimus for remembering padding for the floor. Jupiter quietly brought the double doors together in the middle, leaving just enough space for the two of them to see the chair where the hologram would sit, and part of the window to its right.

Mallory listened as the voices got closer. She could hear the two men's steps as they mounted the second flight of stairs and emerged into the room.

"Spectacular," Draven Chandler said. "A room this big — well — "

"Yes," Septimus said. "It was really this space that sold me on the house."

"Quite a study!" Chandler said. "I see you and I very different work habits. I can't believe how well organized your desk looks. Mine is total chaos. And what's this?" There was silence for a moment. "A Magic 8 ball?"

"Yes, indeed," Septimus said. "It might have been marketed as a child's toy, but I've found it to be remarkably profound. Perhaps my mystical streak allows me greater access to it."

"I'll have to try it again," Chandler said. "I haven't played with one since I was a good bit younger."

Mallory heard his footsteps move away from Septimus' desk.

"I bet during the day you can see to the horizon from these windows," Chandler said.

"You're right, I can," Septimus said. "Step back a bit. The windows have electric shades and I want to close them to block out any ambient light." Mallory heard the whir of the motor as the shades dropped to cover the windows, both in the study and upstairs in the observatory.

"Would you like to sit down?" Septimus asked Chandler.

"What's this?" Chandler asked curiously.

"Oh, just my little collection of Spanish and Mayan artifacts," Septimus said.

Mallory could hear almost everything pretty clearly, but it was a bit frustrating not to be able to see. The two men discussed Spanish armor and Mayan weapons, and Chandler seemed particularly taken with the posters of the Mayan codices.

"I was never as interested in the Spaniards as I was in the Maya," Chandler said. They were on the other side of the room now, and talking in low voices. Mallory was having a hard time piecing together the sentences. She glanced at Jupiter, but he didn't seem to be bothered. She assumed that when things heated up everyone would be louder.

At last Chandler and Septimus sat down just out of sight, and much closer to them.

"So where does this ghost usually show himself?" Chandler asked.

"Over by that chair," Septimus said.

They were silent for a while, as if Chandler were waiting for a spirit to materialize – or at least contemplating the possibility. At last he said, "I can't get over the fact that you bought this house from a Gideon Sawyer. It's not a very common name."

"No," Septimus said. "I don't suppose it is. You mentioned you knew a Gideon Sawyer when you were a child. Where was that?"

"South of here," Chandler said. "Near the sea below San Diego. We both lived on a commune down there. Gideon and I were actually friends for a while, but I lost track of him."

Mallory grimaced. She thought Gideon would probably dispute Chandler's characterization of their relationship.

"A commune?" Septimus asked, with apparent interest. "What was that like?"

"Actually," Chandler said, "that was where I first got interested in the Maya and their belief that there was no real difference between life and death — that life continued beyond death and that you could dwell in the realm of the gods. The Spaniards with their obsessive Catholicism found the Mayan religion baffling and repulsive, with its human sacrifice — although sacrifice is at the heart of Catholicism too, of course."

That was genuinely interesting, Mallory thought. She glanced at Jupiter. He seemed to think so, too.

"The Spaniards mistook human sacrifice for barbarism," Chandler went on. "The Maya practiced it to appease their gods, yes, but they believed in the cyclical nature of life. They believed that nothing ever truly died."

"You're right, of course," Septimus said. "From their astronomical observations, the Maya came to believe that all life was cyclical, and that the eternal round of existence was proven by the cycles of time – the days and nights, the passage of the sun and moon across the sky."

"I can't tell you how refreshing it is to talk with you," Chandler said. "I thought from the start you might be a kindred spirit. Even among people who believe in life extension and the possibility of immortality, the Mayan religion is not wildly popular. There's a lot of revulsion about human sacrifice, but sometimes it seems necessary, don't you think? From time to time? For the greater good?"

The hair on the back of Mallory's neck prickled. So the greater good was being served by the death of Senator Hayden and the attempted murder of Skinny? It seemed that Draven Chandler had mixed up the greater good with what was good for him.

"All people can see is the acts of sacrifice themselves," Chandler said, "but it isn't revolting at all if you understand that the sacrificed went at once to live with the gods."

Like Muslim martyrs, Mallory thought. It was fascinating how the same ideas had circled back again and again since the dawn of human history.

"Stop," Septimus said, all of a sudden. "Did you hear that?"

"Hear what?" Chandler said, his voice eager.

"I thought I heard someone say, 'Hello, Draven,'" Septimus said.

Again the hair stood up on the back of Mallory's neck. She knew that Septimus was starting to open the trap, but still it was spooky.

Chandler's voice was hushed. "I didn't hear it," he said. "Maybe you should turn the light off."

Mallory heard Septimus rise from his chair and walk to his desk. When he turned off the standing lamp, the room was plunged into total darkness. There were noises in the darkness and then Septimus spoke.

"I heard him again," he said, his voice heavy with portent. "This time he said, 'Draven Chandler, I knew you once.'"

"He did?" Chandler said. There was a pause that seemed to go on forever to Mallory. In the stillness and utter darkness, Mallory felt almost disembodied. She reached out and touched Jupiter to make sure he was still there. He took her hand, squeezed it, and then let go.

"Gideon Sawyer," Chandler said softly. "Is that you?"

Again, silence. But slowly, out of the darkness, a ghostly figure began to materialize in the chair that Mallory could see through the crack between the doors. Its colors were faded and tended toward bluish-white. It looked at one and the same moment amazingly solid and a bit hazy, like a cloud of smoke. Still, its features were distinct – wide cheekbones, a square chiseled chin, short reddish-blond hair. It looked almost exactly like Gideon Sawyer – though a bit younger than the man she'd met.

Wow! Mallory thought. Whatever technology Septimus was using was utterly amazing. She was startled when the image moved. Its head turned in the direction of Draven Chandler's voice. "Hello, Draven," it said. "It's been a long time."

"Yes," Chandler said, a bit breathless. It was one thing to generally believe in ghosts, Mallory thought, and something else entirely to have the ghost of an old acquaintance speak to you. "I was sorry to hear that you'd died."

The hologram seemed to chuckle. "As you can see, death is just an illusion."

"I can't believe you lived in this house, so close to where I've been working," said Draven Chandler. "But you never got in touch. I think we were both about ten or eleven the last time I saw you."

"That would have been soon after the

commune came apart," the image said, nodding. "Soon after the death of your father."

"Yes," Chandler said.

"We all knew you didn't really mean to kill him," the hologram said, its voice sympathetic and a touch mournful. "You had a terrible temper in those days."

Chandler's voice became brittle and defensive.

"What do you mean?" he asked. "I didn't kill my father."

"Of course you did," the image said, as if addressing a small child. "Everyone in the commune knew you must have shoved him in one of your fits. What had he said to you? That you couldn't go down into the well any more?" The image gripped the arms of the chair and sat forward.

Chandler said nothing, but Mallory could hear his harsh breathing.

"I didn't kill my father," Chandler said again, but he didn't sound convincing.

"No," the hologram said. "The fall from the cliff killed him. But he wouldn't have fallen if you hadn't shoved him."

"I told you," Chandler said. It sounded like he was gritting his teeth. "I didn't push him. Though I did have a terrible temper, you're right about that. My father just slipped and fell. My mother kept telling him not to get so close to the edge."

"That may be so," the hologram said, "or it might have seemed that way to you. Surely a child's mind would rearrange the facts to make them easier to live with. Still, I think you know more about matters of life and death than you are admitting."

Chandler turned to Septimus. "I swear," he said, a hint of desperation in his voice. "I didn't kill my father." Septimus said nothing. "Is this the same spirit that you saw up here before?" he asked.

"It looks the same," Septimus said, "but it never spoke to me."

Chandler turned his attention back to the hologram. "I do know something about life and death," he said. "That's what my life's work has been."

"What have you discovered?" the hologram asked.

"That life never ends," Chandler said. "I hardly need to convince you of that."

"No," the hologram said. "Though old spirits tend to fade away. Otherwise, it would get quite crowded in the spirit realm."

"What do you mean, 'fade away'?"

Chandler asked.

"Nothing lasts forever," the hologram said. "Immortality is a tale to assuage the endless pain of human loss. But we do have a while still, here on the other side. As a matter of fact, we've recently greeted someone you know."

"Who?" Chandler said, instantly suspicious.

Here we go, Mallory thought. The trap was closing.

"The late senator from California," the hologram said gently. "Jack Hayden. He seems to think that you and someone named Byron Baxter killed him so that you could take his seat in the United States Senate."

Mallory heard a noise like a chair skidding backwards. It seemed Chandler had stood up suddenly and pushed the chair behind him. "Now wait just a minute," he said. "That's a lie, Gideon. We did nothing of the kind. The old man was losing his mind. All we did was enroll him in a drug trial for a drug that might have halted his senility. If it had worked, it would have saved the election for him. It wasn't our fault the drug killed him. Neither one of us knew that it might react badly with some other drugs."

Chandler's voice had risen in tone and volume as he spoke, and by the end, it seemed to be reverberating in the octagonal room. Mallory held her breath.

The hologram seemed to be nodding. "So you say," it said. "But it seems to me that the fact that you even mentioned the drug interactions is as good as a confession."

Chandler didn't respond at first, and Mallory could imagine him staring at the hologram. "A confession?" he said hoarsely. "What do you mean, 'a confession'? Is that what you're after?"

The atmosphere in the room had altered violently. The sense of anticipation and pleasure that Chandler had brought with him at the possibility of meeting a ghost had changed to anger, grievance, and wary self-defense.

"What is this?" he asked. "Is this some kind of trick? Some Victorian parlor game? A séance with an end goal?"

He rushed toward the hologram. Mallory could see him, his arms outstretched, as though he wanted to throttle it. But before he could reach it, Septimus shut it down. The room and the observatory above it were totally black. The faintest light seemed to filter up into the room from the stairs to the second story.

Everything was still for a moment, and then Septimus turned the floor lamp back on and the room was suffused with a dim light. As he began to speak, his voice was low-key, friendly, and pleasant. "You certainly never know what's going to happen in this life, do you, Draven?" he said. "It's one surprise after another."

"Quite a surprise," Chandler said, menacingly.

"My very first ghost," Septimus said with a chuckle, "and it accuses my guest of murder. Not very hospitable, and obviously a ridiculous accusation."

Chandler sounded relieved, less guarded. "I'm glad you see it that way," he said.

But Septimus wasn't finished, and his voice took on a steely edge. "Or is it ridiculous?" he asked. "Did you really have something to do with the senator's death? Did you really enroll him in a drug trial knowing it might kill him?"

Chandler's voice got lower, more rumbly and tense. "Now you're being needlessly provocative," he said. He paused, as if to look around the room. Mallory thought of what they'd said two nights ago about how dangerous a man like Draven Chandler actually was —

a man who had killed twice and tried it another time. It seemed likely that right at this moment he was plotting a way to get rid of Septimus Halfpenny and make it seem like an accident.

She glanced at Jupiter. He had tensed up and looked extremely worried. Obviously he was thinking the same thing.

"What I said before was the absolute truth," Chandler said, trying to make his voice as upbeat as possible. "Believe me or not, as you wish." He yawned. "Still, that was very unpleasant, and it's left me feeling a bit shaken. You said you had an observatory?"

"Yes," Septimus said. "Up that spiral staircase."

"Do you think we could go up there?" Chandler said. "Often when I'm unsettled I look at the stars and they calm me right down – put everything into perspective."

"Certainly," Septimus said. "I'm sorry that was upsetting for you. Let me open the shades." Mallory heard the whir of the motor again, and this time they rose. She could just see an edge of one high window, the stars twinkling through it, and a bit of moon.

"Shall we go up?" Chandler said.

Chandler went first, with Septimus close behind. As soon as they were up the stairs and on the observatory's deck, Jupiter pushed open the closet doors and the two of them crawled out. Mallory crept over to the bottom of the circular stairs and looked up. The moonlight and starlight were dim, but enough for Mallory to see the two figures up there.

Jupiter stood beside her, staring too, his face a mask of determination.

"Do these windows open?" Draven Chandler asked.

Without waiting for an answer, he raised one of the sashes. Cool night air flowed in and down the stairwell.

"There's no walkway," Septimus said. "You can't go out there."

"No," Chandler said. "But maybe you can."

Chandler leapt at Septimus and grabbed him around the neck. Septimus broke free, but Chandler kept after him, grabbed him under the arms, and tried to shove him toward the open window. Mallory heard grunts and groans, and the sound of bodies being knocked against the wall.

She'd only been up there once, but she remembered it clearly. It was one of the most dangerous places for a fight that she'd ever seen. The observatory was very enclosed, higher than it was wide. Only twelve feet across, its eight sides, each with a window, were narrow enough to make the room seem circular.

Eight windows opened onto the dome of the Octagon House's roof, which sloped downward to the wide expanse of the porch roof. The walkway below the windows wasn't more than four feet wide, and its interior edge was surrounded by a flimsy decorative banister, with a polished curving handrail and turned spindles that couldn't have been more than an inch and a half in diameter. If the two men crashed against it, it would surely splinter and they would plunge down the stairwell.

The fight had stopped for a moment. They'd broken apart and were facing each other warily. Mallory could hear their ragged hoarse breathing.

"Draven," Septimus said. "What do you think you're doing?"

"You thought you could trick me, did you?" Chandler said. "What was that thing downstairs? A hologram? Very clever."

Septimus said nothing.

"What I don't understand," Chandler said, "is what your interest is in all this? Why did you get involved? What's it to you?"

Jupiter leapt into action as if he'd been summoned. Septimus had gotten involved because of Jupiter, and Jupiter was not about to let him struggle with Draven Chandler alone.

He rushed to the wall where Septimus's collection of armor and weapons hung and he grabbed the double-bladed Spanish short sword he'd snicked through the air the other day. Holding it in his hand, he raced up the circular stairs – so fast it made Mallory almost dizzy to watch.

From below her, she heard the sound of pounding feet and Pete and Bob appeared. They must have been listening on the second floor, she thought, and had heard the sounds of a scuffle.

Up above, Jupiter had reached the walkway, and Chandler had whirled to meet him.

"You!" he said. "I knew from the minute I saw you that you were trouble." He lunged at Jupiter, but Jupiter moved forward, the blade before him.

"Don't think I won't use this," he said ominously. "Now stand down."

"Stand down?" Chandler said. "Who do you think you are? The police?"

All at once, he rushed Jupiter with a high-stepping kick. His aim was true, and the sword flew out of Jupiter's hand. It fell on the floor, and Chandler reached to pick it up.

"Stay back!" he yelled, as he thrust the blade toward Jupiter's chest.

"Let me up there," Pete said. He tried to push his way forward, but Mallory stopped him.

"No," she said firmly. "It's too dangerous up there with two people, much less three. You'll make things worse. Jupiter and Septimus can handle it."

Pete seemed to understand the truth of what she was saying and stopped.

Unfortunately, as Jupiter moved rapidly backwards, away from the sword tip pointing at his chest, he bumped into Septimus – who was lunging forward to come to Jupiter's aid. While the two of them were trying to get disentangled, Chandler swung the sword and struck a glancing blow.

Though Mallory couldn't see exactly what had happened, from the yell that Septimus let out, it was clear that the blade had caught him somewhere. As he now tried to move backward and out of the way of the enraged man, he called out to Jupiter to get back down the stairs – that he should go first and that Septimus would follow him down.

But as Jupiter moved toward the top of the stairs, Draven Chandler rushed him. Breathing hard, still holding the sword, he tried to pin him against the spindles, but Jupiter dodged, and Chandler stopped just short of breaking through the spindles himself.

Chandler backed up and tried to take stock of the situation. What had begun as a simple struggle between him and Septimus, in which he clearly thought he had the upper hand, had shifted.

He now had two antagonists, and though he might have thought he could beat either one of them, the two of them together were more formidable – and as Jupiter recovered his balance and ran to rejoin Septimus, Mallory could see Chandler move toward the window he'd previously opened.

He hoisted himself on the windowsill and looked over his shoulder. Mallory could see he was gauging the possibility of an escape. In the meanwhile, he was intent on using his legs to kick away anyone who approached him. But suddenly, both Jupiter and Septimus rushed him, side by side, and as Septimus lunged for the whirling sword and Jupiter grabbed his flailing legs, Chandler suddenly lost his balance and toppled backwards out the open window, into the starry night. Mallory heard a loud thump and then a short scream as he hit the house's domed roof and began to slide down it.

As Jupiter and Septimus stood at the window, staring out, Mallory rushed to one of the windows in Septimus's study in time to see Chandler, thrashing and grabbing for a purchase, slide faster and faster down the dome, until he was airborne and flying.

He hit the roof of the porch and crashed through. As Pete and Bob burst into shouts of real alarm, Mallory ran past them and up the spiral staircase. Septimus and Jupiter were still side-by-side, leaning out the window through which Draven Chandler had fallen. Jupiter was so intent on what he was seeing that he hardly noticed her arrival, but Septimus moved back to let her join them, and as she did, she stared down at the gaping black hole in the porch roof.

The body of Draven Chandler lay somewhere underneath it. Was he alive or dead? There were already too many deaths and near deaths for Mallory, so she was extremely relieved when a long low moan drifted up from beneath them. At least he was still alive.

A clatter of feet on the circular stairs and there were Pete and Bob.

"And the match goes to Jupiter Jones!" Pete crowed. He tried to take Jupiter's hand and hold it high, but Jupiter shook his head no.

"And to Septimus Halfpenny," Jupiter said. "Thanks to Septimus, we got Draven Chandler. You did a brilliant job leading him on and drawing him out," he added. "Is your hand all right?"

"It will be," Septimus answered. He was pressing on his palm with his other hand. "Lucky for me, the cut isn't deep. Though for just a moment there I could almost imagine Draven Chandler as a Mayan priest ripping the heart out of his victim at the top of a pyramid. I got the feeling he would have enjoyed that. And now I think we'd better climb down from this eyrie and call both an ambulance and the police!"

15

An Obdurate Outcast

Two days later, Jupiter sat with Bob, Pete, and Mallory in The Three Investigators' outdoor workshop, waiting for Septimus Halfpenny and Gideon Sawyer to arrive. He was still feeling a bit unnerved by the struggle in the observatory of Octagon House. He'd surprised himself with his ability to engage in hand-to-hand combat; he'd always thought that wasn't something he'd be particularly good at. But when it had proved impossible to effectively threaten Draven Chandler with a sword, it had been his only option.

Still, the adrenaline had taken a long time to wear off, and after it had, some shock at the suddenness – and seriousness – of the fight had lingered. Septimus and Gideon were planning to stop by on their way to see a Santa Monica prosecutor, and although Jupiter was grateful that The Three Investigators would be able to largely stay out of the mop-up of everything that had happened, he hoped that Septimus wouldn't end up resenting having gotten involved with the entire complicated series of

294

events.

The night Draven Chandler slid down the domed roof of Octagon House, Septimus actually hadn't called the police in the end — just an ambulance, to take Chandler to the Rocky Beach Hospital, where it had turned out he had broken both of his ankles, and the bones in his left foot. Though he'd slid down the dome pretty neatly, when he'd crashed through the porch roof, he'd ended up landing hard.

Although his bones had been set, even now he was still in the hospital — where Chief Reynolds had visited him to formally charge him with the assault and attempted murder of Septimus Halfpenny. Septimus and Gideon Sawyer's trip to see the Santa Monica prosecutor was to let Septimus deliver a copy of the audio tape to him, and to let Gideon make a statement about Draven Chandler. No one knew yet whether there would be enough evidence to proceed against him and Byron Baxter and Mia Osaka in the case of Jack Hayden, but when Jupiter and his friends had told Chief Reynolds their hypothesis, he had contacted the Santa Monica police.

The good news was that one way or another, Draven Chandler had clearly gone from being a Master of the Universe to being a felon-in-waiting. His presidential dreams were in tatters; he'd have no future as a politician. Someone else would take Jack Hayden's place in the general election that fall.

From Jupiter's point of view, however, the most important thing was that, although Chandler might well retain his authority as an influencer and would certainly remain as the head of the Institute For Eternal Consciousness, as of the moment he attacked Septimus in the observatory of Octagon House, Lief and Magnus's father became completely safe from any threat of a bogus lawsuit or slanderous accusation.

And it turned out – according to Dr. Haldorrson – that Dr. Granger was totally in the clear. When he'd taken the X-rays of Senator's Hayden's foot, he really *had* thought that the old injury had been re-injured, and after he'd fitted him with that big black boot, he'd prescribed him the exact painkiller that was forbidden in the drug trial Hayden was about to be enrolled in.

While Jupiter had no hard evidence that Baxter, Mia Osaka, and Draven Chandler had known what the painkiller was that he'd be prescribed before they came up with their scheme, because of the work she did at the hospital, Osaka knew about the drug trial and the lethal drug interaction – and no doubt they'd had no trouble convincing Senator Hayden that it would be in his best interest to try the drug to improve cognitive function. So when they came up with the idea of the fake foot injury, everything had been in place. And even though Senator Hayden presumably hadn't been in pain, he seemed to have gotten to the point where he pretty much did exactly what his handlers told him to do.

In this case, that had led to a heart attack – and as they waited for Septimus and Gideon Sawyer to arrive, Jupiter, Bob, Pete, and Mallory had been discussing that.

But now the conversation turned to other things. In a few days the the four of them were going up to Ojai for Charlotte Mitchell and Connor O'Malley's wedding. And it seemed that in a couple of weeks they'd be flying to Wyoming. Hector Sebastian had written to Bob the day before to invite the four of them to stay with him and Phillipa Paxton at the ranch where he'd been renting a log cabin. The ranch was outside the town of Dubois, and Hector had offered to buy all four of them round-trip plane tickets to Wyoming, using his frequent flyer miles.

Though this sounded like a lot of fun, and Pete, Bob, and Mallory had all whooped with enthusiasm at the prospect, Jupiter felt a little conflicted. The Three Investigators had only wrapped up three cases so far this summer, and the weeks were speeding by. The last two summers they had managed to investigate six mysteries.

"I don't know," Jupiter said now, to his friends. "Even though our first case of the summer will probably lead to a hefty finder's fee sometime in the coming year, the main point of The Three Investigators is to keep solving cases – and as far as I know, there are no cases waiting for us in Ojai or Dubois."

Pete laughed. "Don't worry. We attract cases like magnets attract iron. They find us wherever we are. And we also seem to be attracting some pretty loyal new friends – Charlotte and Connor, Hector and Phillipa. Imagine someone flying the four of us to Wyoming!"

Just then, a car pulled into the Salvage Yard, and they all got to their feet. Septimus's right hand was bandaged where it had been cut by the sword, but across his shoulder he was carrying a dark blue messenger bag that bulged weirdly. He greeted them all so cheerfully that Jupiter's fear that Septimus might be holding the complicated aftermath of the other evening against him and the others vanished completely.

In addition, as Mallory introduced her friends to Gideon Sawyer, Jupiter had a very positive first impression of Mallory's mother's new boyfriend.

"I'm glad to meet you," Jupiter said. "In the flesh, and not as a light show."

Gideon laughed. "I've just been to see Septimus's house and my hologram," he said. "They both impressed me immensely. Did you know that the dome of the house is modeled on a Roman temple? One of the only houses in the world like that. It's an astonishing building. If you're going to fall down the roof of a building the way that Draven Chandler did, that would be the one you'd want to fall down."

"Gideon's a civil engineer," Mallory told Pete and Bob.

"That's true," Septimus said. "I've hardly ever met an engineer so civil. Polite even."

Mallory laughed, then led the way to the front door of HQ2. Just like Septimus a few days before, Gideon seemed very impressed with it.

"This is great," he said to Mallory. "Very welcoming and airy. And that cupola in the middle of the roof looks a lot like a miniature version of the observatory in Septimus's house – the scene of the downfall of Draven Chandler!"

Mallory looked truly pleased at Gideon's comment.

"I actually based it on a cupola in an American Four-Square kit house owned by a couple we met on a case last summer," she explained to him. "Come on, sit down for a minute." She urged the men toward the formal seating area.

"All right," said Gideon. "But we can't stay very long. I'm told that prosecutors don't like to be kept waiting. Especially in Santa Monica! And we're really here just to give you something. Mallory told me that you have a custom of collecting a memento of each of your cases."

"We sure do," Pete said. "We've got them all exhibited on the back wall." He pointed. "Sort of like Septimus's armor and stuff."

"Septimus and I didn't know if you'd managed to collect one yet – " Gideon went on.

"No," Pete said, his voice rising hopefully. "Not yet."

"Good," Septimus said. "Gideon and I put our heads together and we came up with something. Now don't get too excited. It's something I had on my desk, and both Pete and Draven Chandler commented on it."

"The Magic 8 ball!" Pete shouted.

Septimus smiled. "Both Gideon and I had one when we were young. It's an engineering marvel and a philosophical lesson about life."

He reached into his messenger bag, pulled out a square box, and handed it to Jupiter. Both he and Gideon were grinning broadly.

Pete was familiar with the toy, Jupiter knew, but though he'd heard of it, he'd never had one.

"Numbers were in the air in this case," Septimus said, "with me being the seventh son, et cetera, and my octagon house, and the talk about the Maya and explicit zero. And of course, the number eight on the Magic 8 ball's side is the symbol for infinity. So this seemed appropriate."

Jupiter took it out of its box as Pete, Mallory, and Bob leaned around him. It was a black plastic ball, made to look like an 8-ball in billiards. Jupiter dimly remembered that if you pocketed the 8-ball before it was time to do so, you lost the game. On one side of the ball was a white circle with the number eight in it. On the other side was a round dark glass window. As Jupiter watched, letters seemed to swim up out of the depths of the 8-ball.

"Reply hazy, try again," it said.

"How does it do that?" he asked.

"It's got a viscous blue fluid inside," Gideon explained, "and swimming in that is a 20-sided die with ten positive answers, five negative answers, and five indeterminate answers. You turn the ball up so you're looking at the number 8 and ask the ball a yes or no question. Then you shake it and turn it over. Soon you get your answer."

"It's truly nifty," Septimus said. "I told you I used it to help me make quick decisions. The mother of the guy who invented it was a clairvoyant. He took his inspiration from a writing device she used to communicate with spirits."

"It's been around for over seventy years," Gideon added, "and it's still as fresh as ever. What makes it work so beautifully is the constant human desire for answers. But of course those three possible answers − yes, no, and maybe − are also the answers you get when you formulate a theory or a scientific hypothesis. Yes, the hypothesis is correct. No, it's wrong. Or third, it's not proved."

Jupiter kept shaking the ball and seeing what floated up to the window. "It certainly has a lot of ways of saying yes, no, and maybe," he said.

Septimus laughed in agreement. "'It is certain,' says the 8 Ball. 'Without a doubt.' 'You may rely on it.'"

"Or 'Don't count on it,'" Gideon said. "'Outlook not so good.' 'Very doubtful.'"

"In short," Septimus said, "most of the 8 ball's answers are intended to hedge. While some of the positive answers are unequivocal, most of the rest aren't so clear. And the maybes are doozies. 'Better not tell you now.' 'Concentrate and ask again.'"

"Let me have it," Pete said. He closed his eyes. "Are Connor and Charlotte getting married in a few days?" he asked. He turned the ball over. "'Signs point to yes,'" he read.

"It says they're getting married," he yelled, as if that were truly news. He looked astonished.

"You'd think people would love simple

straightforward answers," Septimus said. "But a lot of the time they like obscure and unclear answers even better. They get to use their imaginations, twist things the way they want them to be. They like that *almost* as much as they love believing things that aren't true at all – like the idea that the Magic 8 Ball can really carry messages from the astral plane.

"Even someone as canny and clever and ruthless as Draven Chandler, with all his cynicism and all his wealth, can have a weakness for believing nonsense, and it can be very hard to resist it," Septimus continued. "Gideon and I hope that this will serve as a memento to remind you four that in the real world there are only truths, untruths, and as-yet-unproven theories."

Though Pete had been listening to Septimus, Jupiter could see he was still in thrall to the Magic 8 Ball.

"I want to ask it some more questions," he said. "Umm, will my soccer team have a winning season this fall?" he asked.

He shook the toy and turned it upside down. "'Don't count on it,'" he read. "Oh, no!"

"Don't worry, Pete," Bob said. "That *can't* be true."

Pete shoved the Magic 8 ball at Jupiter.

"Here," he said. "You ask it some questions. I'm sure it won't lie to you."

The fact that Septimus had come by with a silly gift had put Jupiter in an amazingly good mood, and he was happy to enter into the spirit of the scene.

"O.K.," he said. He stared down at the white circle with the large black 8 in it. "Will The Three Investigators get a new case soon?" he asked. He shook the ball and turned it over. Out of the blue murk, shadowy white letters coalesced, pressing against the window. "'Without a doubt,'" he read.

"There you go," Pete said. "Isn't it great?"

Though Jupiter didn't say so, he thought it was indeed great. In fact, he was oddly excited by the answer, and very bucked up. At the same time it was strange to find himself wanting to believe a totally random answer stimulated by a mechanical action. He thought, and not for the first time, how susceptible the human mind was to what it wanted to hear. He even entertained, for an instant, the idea that a supernatural force had intervened and had turned the die in the blue liquid just so, because it knew the future.

"Let me try again," he said. "Will we run

into the case at Charlotte and Connor's wedding?" Again he shook the ball and turned it over.

"'Very doubtful,'" he read. He felt an unexpected sense of deflation.

"Well, that makes sense," Mallory reassured him. "There's no reason to think we'll stumble on a case at a wedding."

"O.K.," Jupiter said. "Let me rephrase the question. Will we run into a case somewhere in the Ojai valley?"

This time the answer pleased him more. "'Most likely,'" he read, feeling inexplicably happy. He was quite aware of the roller coaster of feelings he'd had, based on accidental answers to arbitrary questions. But the feelings had been real enough, and Jupiter was glad he could keep them to himself.

"So, what do you think?" Pete asked.

"Very interesting," Jupiter said, as noncommittally as he could.

"We're glad you like it," Septimus said. "Though I'm a strong believer in scientific method — which is simply rigorous adherence to the truth and accepting that we are always to some degree wrong — there's something really intriguing about the random. Still, underneath it all is the *logos*."

"The logos?" asked Bob.

"A principle originating in classical Greek thought," Septimus said. "It refers to a universal divine reason that is everywhere in nature, and rises above all oppositions and imperfections in the cosmos. An eternal and unchanging truth present from the time of creation, available to every individual who seeks it. Or so I understand from Socrates."

Although Jupiter might have been imagining it, since Septimus was looking not at Bob, but at Jupiter as he said this, it seemed he was saying this for his ears, mainly – especially because the next thing out of his mouth was, "And though Gideon and I really do have to be going, this has been quite a week for both of us. Meeting new people who seem quite important almost immediately – well, that gets rarer as you get older."

The more Jupiter saw of Septimus Halfpenny, the more he liked him. He had a sharp and agile mind; he was surprising in his interests; and he seemed to consider Jupiter, especially, an equal, not some teenager who was still wet behind the ears. It was great to have a man in his life who had actually known his father – someone with whom Jupiter had a ready-made history, as it were – and just as great to have someone who seemed ready to become Jupiter's mentor.

When he and Gideon stood up and headed for the door, Jupiter and the others walked them to their car. They waved goodbye, then walked back into Headquarters. There, Pete picked up the Magic 8 Ball again.

"Boy," he said. "I wish we could ask it what Bob should name this case. I'm glad we got it as a memento. I thought the memento might have to be the Spanish morrión, but since Septimus gave it to Jupiter, and it's really from his father, I knew he should keep it for himself. As for Bob's title — "

Bob nodded. "I've been thinking about it, of course, and I wanted to ask for your opinions. Because Septimus's house wound up being so important, I thought maybe I'd call it The Mystery of the Octagonal Something-or-Other."

Jupiter frowned. He wasn't at all sure that was a good idea. "What would the noun be?" he asked.

"How about 'oasis'?" Bob asked. "As in *The Mystery of the Octagonal Oasis*? I mean, Septimus's house is sort of an oasis — a place to get away from a very square world. But it doesn't really have much to do with the case, does it?"

"No," Jupiter said. "Why don't we all go home and put our thinking caps on? If any of us comes up with something good, we should let Bob know. Of course, he'll make the final decision."

Everyone agreed that was a good idea, and though Pete had a little trouble parting with the Magic 8 Ball, he, Bob, and Mallory were soon on their bikes and on their way.

Jupiter sat for a moment in HQ2, thinking. Finally, he got to his feet and walked to the office area where the Spanish morrión sat on the desk. He picked it up, cradled it in his arms, and headed back to the house.

There, he took it upstairs to his bedroom where he put it on a shelf he could easily see from his bed. He stared at it for a while, thinking how lucky he was to have an old friend of his father's almost magically appear in his life, right at the proper time.

Of course, it wasn't magic at all, Jupiter thought. It was Mallory being Mallory – careful and dedicated enough to search every single falling-apart box in the oldest and grodiest shed in the Salvage Yard to see if it might actually contain something valuable. It had, and she'd not only found it, she'd known what it was when she did. He'd always be grateful to her for the way she'd brought the helmet and letter to him. It was really Mallory who had delivered Septimus Halfpenny to him – and him to Septimus Halfpenny.

It was amazing, really, to consider that he'd been thinking that very same week that if he could have chosen a parent to be part of his life as he grew from childhood to adulthood, it would have been someone who shared with him a dedication to uncovering the truth. Someone who wanted to ask the big questions.

Jupiter had also liked Gideon Sawyer. He hoped things worked out for Mallory's mother, the way it seemed that Septimus was working out for him. Two new and very interesting men had appeared in their lives, and for Mallory, there was also the new pleasure of the architecture of the Octagon House.

Thinking of Septimus's house reminded him of Bob's proposed title. Jupiter would never say it out loud to Bob, but he thought it was really bad. It fulfilled the need to use the letter "O," but beyond that it really had nothing to do with the case at all. At least, Jupiter didn't think so.

The odd thing was, now that it was over, Jupiter hardly knew what the case had been about – except for helping Dr. Haldorrson and his family, of course. It had involved ghosts and immortality, the Maya and politics, but mostly it had involved a man who was very confused about how to live his life – a man who could scarcely distinguish straightforward truth from straightforward falsehood – never mind the sort of cosmic truth Septimus had mentioned in relation to the *logos*.

That was odd, too, really. What Septimus had said about a universal divine reason found everywhere in nature ran parallel to what Jupiter had been thinking a few days ago about the difference between the kinds of ultimate truths Socrates and other philosophers pursued and the more mundane kind that people ignored, contravened, and infringed upon every day.

Again and again in their cases, Jupiter had seen that if it weren't for the occasional careful *un*truth, a lot of important truths would never have seen the light of day. That had happened in this case, certainly, when Worthington, Jupiter, and Mallory – and also Septimus and Gideon – had all lied their heads off in the service of getting at the truth.

So what would be a good title? Jupiter wondered.

He remembered the first time Septimus

had come to Headquarters and had said that feelings had no business in academia – that intellectuals should concern themselves with the pursuit of truth, no matter where it led, which was often to places that were offensive to many. He'd said that until the Enlightenment, truth was an outcast in most human cultures, and from what he could see, in today's world, it was becoming an outcast again.

What he *hadn't* said, but what was nonetheless true, was that for thousands of years, the brightest minds at universities around the world had debated controversial ideas and opinions in order to uncover the truth. But today the quest for truth had been replaced by the quest for emotional comfort.

Maybe "outcast" would be a good noun for this case, then, Jupiter thought. After all, Septimus himself was now an outcast of sorts – a man who'd been fired from his teaching job for stating an ineluctable truth. Looked at in that way, truth itself often *was* an outcast. Something all too many people seemed to want to shove out of a window – the way Chandler had wanted to shove Septimus. But truth was a very stubborn thing, Jupiter thought.

The morning the whole case started – the morning he'd learned that Senator Hayden had died – Jupiter had been thinking about how he admired the way Bob could use language to gracefully convey complex ideas and tell interesting stories, and the way that Pete responded emotionally to the world around him, to other people and the creatures who lived in it. But he, Jupiter Jones, was interested in something else.

He was interested in getting to the bottom of questions involving truth, and he believed he could do that because, no matter how much people tried to obscure it, it still sat there, stubbornly, waiting to be acknowledged or uncovered.

Stubborn, he thought. But "stubborn" clearly did not begin with an "O."

Since he couldn't think of another word that meant "stubborn," Jupiter went to one of his bookshelves and pulled down an old thumb-eared thesaurus he'd had since he was very young. He opened it and looked up "stubborn."

At once he was reminded why Bob loved the English language. There were so many words that meant "stubborn" – each with its own shadings and nuances.

There was *bullheaded* and *pigheaded*, *stiff-necked* and *headstrong*. Too many seemed to have negative connotations, as if being stubborn –

refusing to be easily swayed – was a bad thing. There was *immovable* and *inexorable, stony,* and *iron-willed.* And at last he came to the synonyms that seemed more positive – *firm, fixed, determined, obdurate.*

Obdurate? he thought. He wasn't quite sure what its connotations were, but it fit the bill – it started with "O."

He pulled out his dictionary and looked the word up. *Obdurate, adj. – unmoved by persuasion, pity, or tender feelings; unyielding.*

That's perfect, he thought. That described truth to a T. With its obsidian eyes and basilisk stare, it had no use for tender feelings. He'd call Bob later and suggest it. But would Bob like it? Although it wasn't certain, Jupiter thought: *Outlook good.*

ABOUT THE AUTHORS

Elizabeth Arthur

Elizabeth was born on November 15, 1953 in New York City. She is the daughter of Robert Arthur, the creator of The Three Investigators series. She was educated at Concord Academy in Concord, Massachusetts, the University of Michigan in Ann Arbor, Michigan, Notre Dame University of Nelson, British Columbia, and the University of Victoria in Victoria, British Columbia.

Before she started working on the New Three Investigators series in December of 2018, Elizabeth spent most of her life writing for adults. *Island Sojourn* – a memoir about building a house on a wilderness island in northern Canada – was published in 1980 by Harper and Row. A second memoir, *Looking For The Klondike Stone*, was published by Knopf in 1992. She is also the author of the novels *Beyond the Mountain, Bad Guys, Binding Spell, Antarctic Navigation,* and *Bring Deeps.*

Elizabeth's writing has received fellowships, grants, and awards from the Bread Loaf Writer's Conference, the Ossabaw Island Project, the Vermont Council on the Arts, and the

Indiana Arts Commission. She twice received fellowships from the National Endowment for the Arts and was the first novelist ever given an Antarctic Artists and Writers Operational Support Grant from the National Science Foundation.

Her novel *Antarctic Navigation* was chosen by the New York *Times* as a Notable Book, received a Critics' Choice Award from the San Francisco *Review of Books*, and was chosen as a Best Book of 1995 by *A Common Reader*. In 1996 the novel received the Ohioana Book Award for Fiction from the Ohioana Library Association.

Elizabeth has also taught creative writing at Miami University in Oxford, Ohio; the University of Cincinnati; and Indiana University/Purdue University of Indianapolis, where she directed the creative writing program. She and Steven Bauer met in 1980 at the Bread Loaf Writer's Conference and have been married since June of 1982.

Steven Bauer

Steven was born on September 10, 1948 in Newark, New Jersey. He was educated at Hanover Park High School in East Hanover, New Jersey, Trinity College in Hartford, Connecticut, and the University of Massachusetts in Amherst, Massachusetts. In 1970 he received a B.A. with Honors in English from Trinity, and in 1975 he received an M.F.A. in English from the University of Massachusetts.

Steven is the author of three books for young people – *Satyrday*, 1980; *The Strange and Wonderful Tale of Robert McDoodle*, 1999; and *A Cat of a Different Color*, 2000. His book of poems *Daylight Savings* was published by Gibbs Smith in 1989 and won the Peregrine Smith Poetry Prize.

Steven's work has received fellowships from the Bread Loaf Writer's Conference and the Fine Arts Work Center in Provincetown, Massachusetts. In addition, he has been given grants and awards from the American Library Association, the Parents' Choice Foundation, the Ossabaw Island Project, the Massachusetts Arts Council, and the Indiana Arts Commission.

From 1979 to 1982, Steven taught lit-

erature and creative writing at Colby College in
Waterville, Maine. From 1982 to 2009 he
taught at Miami University in Oxford, Ohio
where he directed the graduate and under-
graduate creative writing programs. In 2010 he
established Hollow Tree Literary Services, an
independent editing business.